DONALYN MAURER

HONEYSUCKLE'S
fire

Honeysuckle's Fire

Printed in the United States of America

First Printing, 2016

Edited By: LJ & CB Creative Images and Services

Information Address: donalynmaurer@yahoo.com

AHKY-5OVR-46YU-KZ7I

TABLE OF CONTENTS

DEDICATION

To my beautiful little sister,

Angela.

I'm in constant awe of you. I love you.

PROLOGUE

It's early December and the start of my winter break my senior year of college. I'm staring at my Nook trying to concentrate on *Three Wishes*, by Kristen Ashley. I've read it a million times and still it's was my go-to book. I love it almost as much as *Sweet Dreams*.

I smile when the Captain announces the plane will soon be starting its final descent into the Lubbock International Airport. My heart's pounding so fast and hard; almost as if it was going to jump out of my chest and run off. I know exactly where it will run and I'll be close behind it.

Turning my Nook off, I stow it back in my Dooney and Bourke satchel that had been a gift from my big sister, Jaycee, when I started my senior year at UT. The ground comes into view through the clouds as I gaze out the window. Nick told me there wouldn't be much to see with Lubbock being flat. With the winter they'd had, everything would be brown, but I reserved the window seat anyway.

The ground isn't full of brown patches between old red dirt roads, but instead it's a bright white; covered by a thick blanket of snow. The snowstorm that had hit the area the day before had caused a lot of travel delays, so it was good I was arriving today. The roads would be cleared and safer to travel on as he drove the forty miles from his family's ranch to pick me up. Although, he said nothing would stop him from seeing me. If he had to find a snow plow to hijack, he'd be here.

The temperature has already rose back up into the mid-sixties despite the frigid cold the snow storm had brought with it, but that's Texas. Welcome to Texas. Don't like the weather, wait few minutes and it'll change. I smile and shake my head as the well-known saying crosses my mind. It's not out of the norm for Texans to experience all four seasons in the same week and have nothing but heat the rest of the year. Some say it's annoying, but true Texans will always tell you that is what's endearing about our Lone Star State. If we want to experience all four seasons, we travel and then return to our fickle-weathered Texas.

Transferring to Texas Tech my last two semesters has been a huge step for me. After a soul-searching, agonizing two months, in the end, I found it wasn't a difficult decision. Especially when all but two credits transferred. I was close to finishing my degree in animal health science specializing on the business side of things. I will be with Nick even if it means dropping out of college altogether. I know that's extreme and drastic but Nick, my honeysuckle, he is my air. I can't live without him. Breathing has even become difficult when he's not near. I decided I was done going back and forth on whether or not to make the move before getting to know him better. I mean, what rules said we had to know each other for any amount of time before we'd be allowed to fall in love and start our lives? Plus, I'd never been a fan of too many rules, but I was also too scared of my dad, to really walk on the rebel side. I'm happy teetering in between the two and driving all the men in my life crazy. Now, it's Nick's turn.

One night, overwhelmed by my need for Nick, and the fear of losing my independence, I made a horrible mistake. I called Nick and told him I needed time to think things through and then hid myself away for weeks even though he begged me not to. I needed time to refocus myself. We didn't talk at all during that time. Inside, I'd been terrified and felt panicked and unsure but as I hid, I felt lost and lonely. Those days, not hearing his voice, had felt like an eternity in hell.

My grandma had begun insisting I call him or she was. I wasn't able to eat or sleep and all I was doing was crying and moping around. Most of those days, I stayed at my Uncle Brock and Aunt Paige's house and hung out with Callie. She was the only light during that time and it kept me going.

I wanted the comfort of my parents but my emotional state wasn't the best, and I didn't want them to suffer with me. They'd been through enough pain and turmoil during the last couple of years over the loss of our family's patriarch, my grandpa Colton, and over what happened to Jaycee and me. My dad still carried guilt over not recognizing Rocky was dangerous. I could see it still haunted him when he looked at us. He carries a sadness now that breaks my heart. My Uncle Brock knew that what I needed was time to figure things out for myself.

One afternoon my grandma stopped by and saw my condition. I don't think I'd brushed my hair or changed from my pajamas in days. Callie hadn't even been able to shake my mood. Grandma told me if my heartbreak wasn't enough proof that I should be with Nick, then nothing ever would be.

"Sweetheart," she'd said to me. "This love came in and knocked you over, leaving you stunned. I understand that it surprised you, but just shake off the shock and go with it. Be happy you never have to go searching. Feel blessed that love found you. Nick found you." Her wise words convinced me to call Nick.

When I finally called, Nick didn't answer. For two days I called and called. I left messages, one in the morning telling him I was wrong and how sorry I was. One in the afternoon telling him how much I missed him, and one at night, wishing him sweet dreams and telling him I loved him. I asked him to get in touch with me, but nothing came of my pleas. My phone never rang once. I knew I'd waited too long; I'd pushed him too far away and lost him. But on the third day, after hearing nothing and having given up all hope, my phone rang. When I saw it was Nick, my breathing became heavy. I was terrified he was going to tell me to leave him alone and stop calling. The finality had me clutching my chest because I wasn't exactly sure what was waiting for me when I answered. Taking a deep breath calmed my panic enough to say hello.

"Please, be ready to come to me, darlin'," his pained voice whispered, causing my knees to buckle as I let out a sob. He had been hurting just as much as me.

"Yes," I simply whispered through my tears. During our call, we had made our plans.

Nick calls me his fire but now that I've learned of his betrayal, my fire is dead.

As the night falls deeper and darker, I sit with my thoughts. If I make it out alive, can I believe in us again? Will I ever believe in him again? Will I be able to forgive him? All I can do now is pray I'll be found before the wind, chill and dark make me lost to him, to everyone forever. Or I can pray for death to end all my pain. Soon, I find myself praying for the latter.

CHAPTER ONE

My sister is always teasing me about Nick replacing pizza as my number one most favorite thing in the world. I joke back saying nothing could ever take away the coveted number one spot from pizza, but that's a lie.

Now, my top ten list of things I love are all something to do with Nick. From his slightly curly blonde hair, to his five o'clock shadow and bourbon colored eyes, to the way he can fill out denim jeans. His snap down western shirts always fit snug against his broad chest like they're tailor-made for him. Nick could be the poster boy for what a good ol' country boy looks like. His southern charm, stubborn ways and cocky attitude, along with his body and the way he dresses, scream county. There's nothing about Nick that I don't love. Mostly his smile, laugh and bossiness. Those things are my air, water and shelter. The things I need to survive. From the day he saved my life, I became his and although I was confused for a time, I can't wait to start my life with him.

Though I'm the baby of the family, the runt as my brothers call me, I had no fear standing up to my dad, Stone, and my four older brothers, Jake, Jesse, Nash and Chase. Even with my uncles Duke and Brock and cousin, Bradley, thrown in for good measure, I stood my ground and fought for Nick and I.

I even went so far as to promise my dad that nothing would go wrong. I was taught promises are something you should never ever give if there's a sliver of doubt you intend on breaking it. A promise is a promise. It is to be kept.

My mom, Violet, and aunts Savannah and Paige, my sister, Jaycee and grandma, Lila, have been all about the romance of my relationship with Nick. They support my decision to move to be near him. I plan on doing a lot of traveling back and forth from Lubbock to San Antonio and Comfort over the next few months to help Jaycee plan her wedding and the move into her new home. I'll only be about four hours from them.

Not being near Jaycee is something I know will hit me the hardest. I'm really going to miss her, but her life with Blue is beginning and they need their time. Like it or not, our relationship is going to take a backseat to theirs, as it should. My relationship with Jaycee won't suffer; it will just be different.

My dad has his construction company working around the clock to finish their home by March. The entire family is pitching in so it will be done in time for the blooming of the blue bonnets. Since Blue really wants Jaycee to have that beautiful memory, my dad blocked off a couple of months to get it finished. He pushed back other jobs and turned down others so he could focus on it. Blue and Jaycee aren't marrying until June, but were already living together with Grandma. After everything she's been through the last year, she deserves all the beauty everyone wants to give her.

Callie, my second-cousin, who calls me Aunt Abby, I already miss and it's only been a few hours. My sister and brothers Nash, Jesse and Jake were adopted by our grandparents, they're legally considered Callie's aunt and uncles but Chase and I are still her second cousins. When she began calling us Uncle Chase and Aunt Abby, my uncle Brock and Aunt Paige urged us to let it be.

"As she gets older, we'll be able to explain our family's confusing dynamics but for now, let it stand as is." Uncle Brock had said.

Last night, I cried when I tucked Callie in tight after reading her Sleeping Beauty. Every night, without fail, she picks the book Jaycee gave her as a 'welcome to the family gift' as her bedtime story. Still to this day, it's my favorite fairytale as well as Jaycee's. Halfway through, Callie fell asleep but as usual, I kept reading until the end. Before leaving, I kissed her cheek and tucked her in snug and made my way downstairs to Uncle Brock and Aunt Paige. They both saw how upset I was and told me that they'd bring her up soon to see me. Callie's brother, Linc, who is also Nick's good friend, lives close to where I will be living so it will be easy to visit.

Everyone was in shock to learn that Callie and Cole were Linc and Rocky's brother and sister. They shared the same father but had different mothers. Strangely, we have become one big family. The Jennings, Bradshaw and McGinty's and now we'll add the Callaghan's.

After Rocky attacked and almost killed Jaycee and me, we learned that his dad, Dr. Jennings, had been blackmailing him. To stop Dr. Jennings from hurting Lincoln and Lina Jennings, Rocky's brother and mom, he agreed to take experimental drugs. At times, he was given them without his knowledge. Dr. Jennings and a few others were attempting to create a new drug for pain, but it turned into nothing more than something to get high on and make them money. One that would make all those greedy bastards rich. It led Rocky into the dangerous world of drug dealing and mental illness where he became trapped within the dark of his mind. It damaged Rocky mentally, but mostly emotionally, when he realized all the hurt and pain he'd caused. After Dr. Jennings was murdered and could no longer hurt or drug Rocky, he realized what he'd done. The guilt over the pain he'd caused haunted him and kept in him the dark. In the end, the real Rocky stepped out of the shadows in time to save Jaycee, Callie and Aunt Paige from an attack. A crooked cop and his thugs invaded my grandma's and attempted to kidnap Callie to flush Rocky out. Rocky was shot in the process of protecting them; he took a bullet meant for Callie and Jaycee. Before the ambulance took him away, my sister and everyone who was there showed him kindness and forgiveness. Rocky was granted redemption. In the end, he finally had peace from the nightmare life he'd been living.

We also learned Callie's mom, Sasha Rowe, was a beautiful loving mom to Callie. She, like so many others, was a victim to Dr. Jennings' sick and twisted mind. Detective Walters and Sergeant Taylor informed us there was much more to her story; information they'll share with our family, but they have to wait until the investigation is complete. They did hint that Callie's mom died trying to protect Callie.

Now, three months later, I've packed my bags and jumped on a plane. Finally, I'm going to be with Nick.

I'll be attending the Texas Tech campus but plan on living with him. He has a cabin about a mile from his parent's main house on their ranch; a half hour drive from campus. I planned on moving into the dorm, but he put a halt to that idea before all the words were even out of my mouth.

I packed all my things that I couldn't carry on the flight in boxes and my dad promised to bring them up soon. Nick's cabin is fully furnished so we'll have everything we'll need, but the word "cabin" has me doubting that. I just hope it at least has a nice bathroom and kitchen.

"Darlin', bring clothes or don't. I promise you won't be needing them for a while anyway." A smile spreads across my face at the memory of Nick's promise. Apparently he plans on keeping me naked in bed for a long time and I'm happy to oblige him.

As the plane touches down and makes its way down the taxiway to the gate, I close my eyes trying to calm myself. I jump up and grab my carry-on and satchel as soon as the Captain gives the 'okay' over the speaker and speed walk off the plane.

Making my way up the jet way, my heart starts beating faster. When I turn the corner to the gate, I'm ready to break into a light jog or full out run to the baggage claim where Nick will be waiting.

Reaching the gate, I stop briefly to look for directions but my search ends when my eyes land on the hottest looking cowboy wearing a denim coat and a beautiful smile.

Nick has somehow got through security and is waiting for me. Standing tall, his hands are tucked in his front jean pockets and he's smiling at me. I drop my things and take off running. He pulls his hands from his pockets just in time to catch me when I jump into his arms.

"Hey, darlin'," he whispers into my neck.

I raise my face up to him and smile. "Hey, honeysuckle," I whisper back.

I kiss the hell out of my cowboy in the middle of the small Lubbock airport not giving a damn who can see us.

CHAPTER TWO

We pull my bags from the belt at baggage claim and hightail it to the exit. A blast of cold wind hits me as we step out into the parking lot and my hair starts whipping around. I pull my coat together with one hand and try holding my long blonde hair back with the other. The Texas sun is shining bright and between wind gusts, I feel its warmth. The wind is like ice though, making it feel so much colder than it is. There's still quite a bit of snow on the ground but here at the airport, it looks dirty as it turns to sludge. This is the ugly side of snow, the part not on postcards or in Hallmark movies. *Yuck*, I think before my eyes travel back to Nick and hone in on his fine backside, switching that thought to, *yum.*

My man doesn't just have a nice butt he has a fine ass. He leads me to an old beat up two-toned blue and white Chevy Silverado. It's retro and instantly I'm in love with it. I had to leave my VW bug back in San Antonio because my dad and Nick didn't want me making the four-hour drive alone. My eyes roll at the memory of our argument about it. I'm almost twenty-four years old; it's totally ridiculous how they treat me at times, when people younger than me are backpacking across Europe, going away to college and driving home on the weekends. Many of my friends are married with children and actually holding down jobs. *Go figure.* I roll my eyes to myself again. But me, I can't make the four-hour drive from home to here? Rather than argue and waste time, I conceded and agreed to wait and pick it up next time I'm in town with Nick. Nick told me I could drive his Jeep that he has anytime I wanted so there's no rush. When we make it to his truck, he sets my two suitcases down and pulls me to him.

"Abigail, these last few months have been shit without you. I'm so fucking happy you're here," he says as he leans in and kisses me.

I forget about the cold and kiss him back as he pulls me closer. I slide my hands under his coat and wrap my arms tight around his waist, never wanting to let go.

"Let's get back. Tonight, we have to go pick out a Christmas tree," he says as he releases me and opens the passenger door.

Nick helps me into the cab of the truck. "Christmas tree?" I ask, as a huge smile spreads across my face. I hadn't even thought about Christmas. My thoughts have been so consumed with missing Nick, then making my way to him, that I'd completely forgot.

"Yes, ma'am. Our first of many. This year we start traditions. Ones that will get passed down generation after generation. Then there are the ones that will be just ours, like making love under the tree, so we got to get on it." he says and winks.

"Yes we do," I giggle.

Nick closes my door, walks around to the driver's side and leans in to start the truck.

"The heater should kick on pretty soon with warm air. Be right back."

But before he can exit the truck I lean across the distance separating us and kiss him again. He deepens the kiss, one of his hands finding the back of my head, holding my lips close to his. I sigh and he moans, each letting the other know how much we missed this during our time apart. Pulling back slowly, I open my eyes and take in his handsome face for a few moments while reminding myself he's really mine.

"We need to hurry. I can't wait much longer to have you, darlin," he says.

I can't help the whimper that leaves my lips as I sit back, still keeping my eyes on him. He grins before getting back out of the truck and closing the door. He rushes to secure my luggage with some rope and a tarp he pulls from a toolbox stored in the bed. He gives one last tug on the rope testing the tightness so my luggage won't fly out the back, before hopping back in the truck. He reaches over and grabs my hips, pulling me so I'm next to him. "I brought my truck because it has a bench seat and I could have you up against me. Now, fasten your seatbelt and hold on while I break every traffic law between the airport and the ranch so I can get you to myself." he says and shifts the truck in gear.

On the highway, the roads are mostly empty with only a couple of other vehicles traveling like us. Laying my head on Nick's shoulder, I breathe him in. God, I missed him so much. He pulls my hand to rest on his thigh and we lock our fingers tight for the drive to the ranch.

CHAPTER THREE

I lean against Nick and watch the scenery as we drive. Fields of snow with oil wells pumping slowly up and down fly by while I absently rub my thumb along Nick's inner thigh. Only when he squeezes my hand do I look over at him in question.

"Hey, darlin', reach down and turn on the radio. I need a distraction from my thoughts or this is going to be a very uncomfortable ride." he says.

I laugh and then look down and see the radio is the only thing new in the truck.

"You got it, honeysuckle."

"Love when you call me that, Abigail."

I push the power button and the light for the CD is showing and flashing reading so I lay my head back on his shoulder. "I love you, Nick." I whisper.

All of a sudden, Nick pulls the truck to the side of the road and stops. I look over at him, startled, when he puts the truck in park. He turns his upper body around and reaches over and unbuckles my seatbelt, pulling me onto his lap. He grabs my face with his hands and brings me in close for a passionate kiss.

"I love you too, Abigail, my fire." he whispers against my lips.

I lose all control, straddling and kissing him, not holding back. We break apart and laugh when the CD starts playing, *Boogie Shoes*. Nick grins before tapping my thigh.

"Let's get back."

I climb off his lap, situate myself back in my seat and fasten my seatbelt while Nick leans down and turns the stereo way up before pulling back onto the road. For the rest of the drive, Nick and I sing along with KC and The Sunshine Band.

It takes almost thirty minutes before we pull off the road and turn into a private drive that's shaded by tall ash trees. I get jostled around the truck as we cross a cattle guard but my eyes are focused on a tall iron arch that reads, Callaghan Ranch. Est. 1913. My eyes fly to Nick before I look back and see it has an automatic iron gate that's closing. Stone walls line the first few yards on either side of the arch, before turning into white wooden fencing with a few horses standing around in the snowy pasture. He keeps traveling down a gravel drive and soon we pass a clearing where a huge two-story white house with balconies running along both floors sits behind a paved drive. There's a Volvo and a Lincoln Navigator, both black parked out front, but Nick doesn't stop there. My eyes travel from the house and cars to the road and then back at him. I wait, but he says nothing. He never once let on that he came from money. When he said his family had a ranch I *assumed* they had a few horses and cows, maybe even a goat and possibly a couple of chickens, but this? I never imagined this.

As we travel down the road we pass more wide pastures, huge stables and animal shelters and I can see the tops of what I think are barns. There are smaller trails leading off the main road.

"Nick?"

"You're freaking out. That's why I didn't tell you. It's not important," he says when he sees my mouth is hanging open. We come to a stop in front of a large cabin with a huge porch and chimney off the side of it. I scan the area and spot a huge, red bloodhound. My eyes widen as it lift its giant head up off the porch and I look at Nick, mouth still hanging open. When I hear a howl my head flies back to the cabin and the dog. Very slowly, and I mean very slowly, the dog rises up and clumsily makes its way down the porch steps and over to the truck.

"Come on. I want you to meet Elvis. Buford is around here somewhere," Nick says while glancing around. He opens the door and steps out but when I don't move, he reaches back in the truck, undoes my seatbelt and slides me across the seat and out the driver's side. He kisses me quickly and sweetly before setting me on the snowy ground.

"This is Elvis," he tells me, rubbing the dog behind the ears. I swear Elvis is smiling up at Nick but when he looks over at me he stops and narrows his eyes.

Now, he looks harmless enough and kind of goofy, but hounds are big dogs so I'm not sure if I should be scared or not.

"Elvis, be good. This here's Abigail and she's staying, so get used to her." Nick orders as squats down. "You're both my girls." he says and she licks his face.

"What?" I ask, shocked. "Elvis is a girl?" I stare at Elvis who has just put her nose in the air as if to say, "That's right, a girl."

Before I can comment further, there's a commotion and I turn just in time to see a huge St. Bernard come out of the trees galloping towards us. *Oh, my God!* It's not going to stop. I stand back as it jumps up on Nick and starts licking his face. Its white fur with brown spots is shaking in glee as Nick rubs his head while laughing and trying to avoid its kisses.

"Abigail, meet Buford," Nick says.

As if Buford knows proper manners, he plops down on all fours and walks over to me, looks up and appears to smile. I carefully reach down and start rubbing his head and he relaxes into me, almost knocking me over.

"Keep your feet planted when you're around these two. They don't mean to but they can knock you over." I'm smiling back at Buford while listening to Nick when out of the corner of my eye, I notice Elvis moving closer to me. When she gets to me, she lets out a sigh like she's exhausted and hasn't just been resting on the porch. I push Buford back a bit and squat down and start rubbing Elvis behind the ears too. She lets out a groan, closes her eyes and drops to the ground. She huffs, and then I hear soft snoring.

Ah, a lazy girl just like me. Yes, Elvis, we're going to get along just fine.

"Alright, enough. Let's go," Nick says as he grabs my hand and helps me stand. As soon as I do, he leans down and picks me up, throws me over his shoulder and turns towards the cabin. I'm laughing as he walks up the porch steps and I get one last glance at Elvis and Buford who are both lying down, chin to the ground watching us with curious but sleepy eyes. Before Nick closes the door, I hear synchronized snoring coming from them and I can't help but laugh harder as I hold on to Nick's butt trying to steady myself.

CHAPTER FOUR

I'm still laughing while hanging upside down, watching Nick's fine ass as he walks through the cabin and makes his way down the hall. He stops beside a bed, and I start feeling a little nervous, but when he pulls me back up and gently slides me down the front of his body, all my apprehension leaves. I look into his beautiful bourbon colored eyes, and my nerves settle as peace and warmth fill me.

Taking the lead, I reach up and push his denim coat off his shoulders and slide it down his arms until it falls to the floor. My hands travel up his dark brown western shirt. I can feel the heat radiating from his skin through the material of his shirt causing his breathing to become heavy as he groans from my touch. Rising up on my tiptoes, I kiss him, our tongues touching briefly before I pull back. Reaching down, I yank his shirt from his jeans and pull it apart, the snaps popping open easily. I sigh and he hisses as I run my hands up the front of his chest that's been softly darkened by the sun. He has a light smattering of hair that travels down into his jeans and I run my finger along its path causing him to grip my hips tightly.

Leaning in, I place a kiss over his heart and when my tongue tastes him, I moan. He steps back and yanks his shirt off causing my breath to catch. His tanned, strong shoulders bunch with his movements making my knees become weak and my eyes hooded. Now he comes for me. Stepping in close, he pushes my coat down my arms and tosses it aside. I watch it land near his and then wait for his next move. His hands rest on my hips while his eyes travel down my body, widening as he takes in my fuzzy pink sweater showing just a hint of skin between my belly button and low rise Wranglers. Seeing that, he reaches out and runs his fingers along my skin, spreading goose bumps along their path before stopping near my belt buckle. Although I've spent a lot of time in Nick's arms, we've only been together once and the need to feel him is stunning me.

Nick pulls my sweater up and off me and tosses it aside. He takes in a deep breath and again traces the pink lace running along the mounds of my breasts. That's right. I wore the sexiest bra and panties I could find. I went to Victoria's Secret on a mission of finding the perfect set for Nick and from the look on his face, he's appreciating my effort. His fingers make their way from my breasts, down my stomach where he circles my belly button before going back and gently tracing a path along the waist of my pants and stopping on my belt buckle. I gasp in a breath and my hands fly to his shoulders when he yanks it open roughly, my body jolting from the force, my breathing becoming heavy. Damn, that was unexpected but hot.

"Stand still, fire." he mumbles his order as he flicks open the snap of my jeans and yanks my zipper down. "Fuck me." he hisses when he sees the top of my matching pink panties.

All of a sudden I'm on my back, lying sideways across the bed and Nick is undressing me. He yanks off my boots and socks and doesn't stop until he's rid me of my jeans. My breath hitches when he stands to his full height, taking one more look down my body, before coming down on top of me.

"Beautiful and fucking mine, finally," are his last words before his mouth is attacking mine. His hands go into my hair, his fingers tightening in the strands while he holds my head immobile and devours my mouth. I wiggle under him until he rises up slightly and I pull my legs out from underneath him, wrapping them around his waist while never breaking our kiss. My hips meet his and I can feel how hard he is through the denim of his jeans. I can't help the whimper that escapes my throat when I feel his heat and my hands fly to his butt pulling him closer. I'm no expert on the male anatomy, seeing I've only slept with one other guy during my freshman year of college, Joey. He was sweet and I thought we were in love and would eventually marry but both our feelings changed over time. Sex was good with him, but not great, which I learned after being with Nick just once. We were on a completely different level both physically and emotionally. When he undressed and I got a good look at him, I was actually scared. Nick has got to be on the larger than average size on the chart. He took his time, being so sweet and careful because I was still healing from being stabbed by Rocky. Now that I'm healed, Nick is showing his hunger for me and he's not going to hold back, thank God!

When his lips leave mine and start to travel down my cheek to my neck and shoulder, I try reaching between us to undo his belt but he releases my hair and reaches down between us, taking both my wrists and pulling them above my head, locking them down with one hand while the other continues its path. His finger trail across the lace of my panties, teasing me.

"Nick, please," I plead. "I want you. I need you," I whisper while turning my head as he kisses his way down my throat to my breasts.

"Not yet, darlin." He lowers his lips to my breast giving my nipple a soft bite through the lace causing me to moan and shudder.

"Nick. Please!" I softly scream and lift my hips to rub against him, but he keeps up his torture.

"Still, Abigail. Keep your hands where they are. Want a taste of you first," he says as his lips travel down my stomach. He teases my belly button with his tongue, causing me to wiggle around trying to get loose of his hold.

I'm trying to do what he says but when I feel his breath on me through the lace of my panties; I break free of his hold, tangle my fingers in his hair and hold him where I need him. "Nick!" I scream and he lets out a deep chuckle.

He rises back up and rips my panties down my legs and then he's back, his breath and tongue hot on me. It only takes seconds before I explode. He growls as he helps me ride out my orgasm until I collapse on the bed. When my eyes can focus again, I see he's standing over me, undoing his belt buckle and unsnapping his jeans. I lick my lips knowing what's waiting and wanting a taste. I've only done that once before with my ex and it was a total fail. I had no idea what I was doing. Apparently you don't 'blow' on it even though it's called a 'blow job'. Who knew? That experience scarred me and I never tried again, but now, looking up at Nick, I'm willing to try again and again. I rise up on my elbows but Nick quickly and gently puts his hand on my stomach and pushes me back down.

"No. No way. Not now. Won't last and I want inside you," he rasps as he leans down and pulls off his boots and pushes his jeans down. He's gone commando and seeing him up close in all his glory is making me squirm because I'm more than ready. He takes me in as he pulls my knees apart and smiles before coming down on top of me and kissing me as he undoes the clasp on my bra and pulls it down my arms before tossing it behind him. He grins before our bodies and lips touch again and his warmth engulfs me.

His fingers make their way to tease me, making sure I'm wet and ready before positioning himself at my entrance and sliding all the way in, in one smooth movement. He gives me a minute before he begins moving and I can't help but feel like I'm melting underneath him. It's a tight fit but and a little uncomfortable but I don't care. It feels like I'm home. Nick is my home now. I need him. All of him and now. He senses my need and must feel the same because he thrusts in me hard and deep. We both gasp at the sensation before he stops; trying to hold back.

"Move, honeysuckle," I say and wiggle my hips.

"Feel okay? I'm not hurting you?" he asks as I run my hands around to his back and up his neck. He's shaking, trying not to hurt me, to be gentle with me, but I need him to take me. Reclaim me. Save my life again.

"Yes, Nick. Take me," I whisper against his ear before softly kissing him there. With that, he pulls back and pushes back into me and we both moan as he keeps going, slow, deep and hard. God, he feels so good. Yes, I need to feel him. I need to know he wants to take me as badly as I want to be taken. He brings his lips back to mine and we kiss, deep and wet. Our bodies slide together easily with our hips meeting forcefully. He's getting close and my body reacts. My muscles begin tightening and I bring my hands to his back and dig my nails in before softly dragging them down and across the muscles. When he moans and shudders, I dig them in deeper causing him to go up on his hands and slam into me.

"Fuck!" he growls and looks down at me while keeping his pace. The more I dig my nails in, the harder he thrusts. Needing him, I'm sure I draw blood. With one hand, I reach down and circle myself while he arches his back so he can see. When his hand comes down and covers mine, deepening my touch, our touch, both of us watch. His large tanned hand over my smaller fair one moving together. That's all it takes, my back arches and I call out his name as I go over the edge and come hard. Our connection is so strong, powerful and beautiful that it overwhelms me and I start to cry. He pumps into me a few more times before groaning through his climax and dropping to his elbows, his head bowed forward against mine. The sweat from his face trickles onto me and I love it.

"Did I hurt you, darlin?" he asks and collapses on top of me.

"No. Not at all. Did I hurt you? I'm sorry about your back." I say as he kisses my neck before making his way back to my lips, shaking his head telling me I didn't. "I love you, Nick. It scares me how much," I confess as the tears fall from my eyes and drop off my cheeks onto the pillow. "It's intense. Sometimes it almost feels too intense," I mumble against his lips as I wrap my arms and legs around him tight while my body shakes with tiny sobs.

"Abigail, I love you and it scares me too because I don't know what I would do without you. I don't think I'd be able to survive and that terrifies me. Those days I didn't hear from you, nothing I did, nothing, could get you out of my head. I almost destroyed myself. You're so deep in my heart it doesn't beat when you're not near. I'm a dead man," he admits.

He slides from my body and falls to my side with his arm around my stomach and pulls me to him. On our sides, facing each other with his arm around my waist, I hitch my leg and drop it over his hip, bringing myself as close as I can to him. We lie like this, just staring in each other's eyes as his fingers wipe my still falling tears. Eventually, my eyes start fluttering closed. Nick kissing me softly on my lips is the last thing I remember before I fall asleep.

CHAPTER FIVE

I awake to warm puffs of air in my face and my nose crinkles at the smell. It smells like bacon, and coffee? It's not exactly bad but it's definitely not good. I open my eyes and squint at the light coming in from the windows. All of a sudden, a very large tongue licks my face and I yelp and try to turn over and wipe my face, but freeze when I feel the bed begin shaking and my body bouncing up and down on the mattress. I smile when I spot Elvis looking down at me.

"Hi, pretty girl."

I reach up and rub her face. She suddenly drops down and plops her heavy head on my stomach and I swear she's already snoring. I think she fell asleep before her head hit my body. I laugh but quickly stop when I hear a deep, soft bark. Turning my head against the pillow, Buford's giant face is staring at me. He's resting his chin on the mattress, waiting.

"The more the merrier. Hop on up, Buford."

I pat the bed and he looks at the bedroom door and stares for a couple of seconds before walking around to the other side of the bed, stopping to look back at me for confirmation.

"It's okay, boy. Come on." I pat the bed. He lets out a deep sigh before hopping up and making his way to me, his eyes darting back and forth between the door and me.

"Buford, are we doing something we're not supposed to be doing?" I whisper to him.

He huffs before dropping and burying his face in my neck. "Ew, gross," I laugh as his cold, wet nose touches my skin. I pet him with one hand while patting Elvis with the other. I'm practically falling off the bed after making room for the two of them but I don't mind. I snuggle into them and all three of us let out a sigh and relax.

"Seriously?" Nick's standing in the doorway with his hands on his hips.

I wrap one arm around Elvis and one around Buford and pull them close to me and smile at Nick.

"Oh, my bad. Is this not allowed?" I ask, playing innocent. Buford and Elvis are looking at Nick but then turn back to me in question. "He's the boss." I give them one final pat and they reluctantly slide from my arms and crawl off the side of the bed. They both slink across the room before making their way through the door

"Abigail." he says in annoyance but laced with humor. I only smile and shrug my shoulders.

CHAPTER SIX

"Come on, troublemaker," Nick says smirking. My eyes follow him as he makes his way over to me with a mug of coffee and sets it on the nightstand. "Want to go get that tree?" He leans down and kisses me.

"YES!" I squeal and move to exit the bed, but quickly remember I'm naked, my eyes darting around searching for clothes. Not getting a good look at the inside of the cabin when we came in, I sit back and my lips part in a small gasp as I take it all in. I didn't expect the inside to look like this with the outside presenting itself as a log cabin, a nice one, but still a log cabin. Lord have mercy, this place is stunning.

Nick's bedroom is gorgeous. The furniture is a mixture of dark wood and gray slate stone across the tops and the bed frame is enormous. It must be at least four feet high along the headboard. I've never seen anything like it. It has to weigh a ton. Come to think of it, when Buford and Elvis hopped on the bed, only the mattress shook, not the frame. Just to be sure, I jiggle around on the bed. Nope, nothing, not even a squeak. Nick's eyes are lit with humor and curiosity as he watches me.

Along the back wall of the room, it's mostly windows. Three sections of tall arched windows in the center with two more smaller but just as tall windows off to the side. Despite the dark wood of the furniture, the room is bright with cream colored walls and a slightly lighter shade of plush carpeting. The windows are draped with beautiful shimmering Delta-colored panels and a wide valence runs along the top. Except for a large mirror that sets directly across from the bed, the rest of the room is bare. Nick returns my earlier shrug of shoulders, playing innocent.

"Are you a king or something?" I ask half joking and half serious.

I plop back on the bed and let out a sigh. I'm completely thrown off. Right when I think I just need time to take it all in, my eyes land on an amazing crystal chandelier that reminds me of a royal crown hanging from the ceiling. With that, I roll over and bury my face in pillow. My Nick, I had no idea.

"Darlin, are you okay?" he asks and I feel his weight fall next to me on the bed. He reaches over and pulls my hair from my face and I blink a couple of times before noticing he looks scared. "Abigail, talk to me." he says softly while pulling me up into a sitting position, facing him.

"Nick, are you sure? Me? It's just, it seems, I don't know. Maybe you should look for someone..." I look down and trail off. My head flies up when Nick all but yells at me.

"Fuck, Abigail. There is no one else for me. I love you," he says and lets out a sigh. "You know I'm older than you, right? I'm close to seven years older than you, darlin'. I've lived more and still I have never, and I mean never, brought anyone back to the ranch. I'm the one who's wondering if you should look for someone, I don't know, closer to your age." He looks down and shakes his head before continuing.

"Abigail, you don't know this about me but until you, I didn't believe in love and relationships. I went out, had some fun but I've never dated. Didn't want kids or a wife. I don't know why I was that way. My parents have a good marriage, a great one and are happy. They've been married thirty-two years and have set a good example, yet, here I am, almost thirty and single. I'm the only child and they're past the point of wanting grandchildren." I listen quietly again, never ever guessing this about him. He always seemed like a 'sweet forever love kind of guy.' When he lifts his head, I see the intensity in his eyes and find myself scooting closer to him on the bed and reaching for his hand. He takes mine and squeezes it.

"I'm not sure when it happened. When I got to you that day at the cabin, and you looked up at me with your big brown eyes, terrified, needing me, trusting me. It opened up a part of me, in my heart and soul. I had no idea that part of me even existed. I sat next to you on the helicopter and not since I was a kid have I bowed my head and prayed, but that day I did. I begged God to make sure you got through it. For the first time, I comprehended its depth and power. As I saw you get better, I kept praying. I've been praying every day since. I prayed while sitting next to you in your hospital room. I somehow knew, I knew *you* were going to be what brought me to the person I am trying to be, whether I wanted it or not. I began wanting more and now I want it all, Abigail. I want you, kids, and grandkids. I never wanted to work this ranch. I resented it and its legacy that would rest solely on my shoulders. I fucking hated it. Then one day, it was the second day exactly, only the second day, I watched you while you were asleep in your hospital bed. I sat across from you, my eyes never leaving you as you dreamed. Like a ton of bricks were dropped on me, I suddenly needed to be able to see you like that every day. I didn't even know you, Abigail. Not really. I didn't know your dreams, but still, I sat staring and my mind drifted into dreams of my own, ones I never imagined. I saw you pregnant with our children. I saw my son and I walking through the pastures of this ranch, teaching him about it, feeling proud. As he got older, riding along the property talking about life, the weather and women as we repaired fencing. Sharing a beer when the time came. I felt what my dad must feel. I saw our daughter, I saw her, darlin' and she looks just like you. I saw her as a little girl, long blonde hair and big brown eyes. She was up on my shoulders while I walked through the barn, talking to the horses. I saw you teaching her how to cook and I saw me walking her down the aisle when she got married. I saw it all. It shocked and terrified me all at once. I even left that night," he says in an agonized whisper.

"I walked away from you. I was going to run away. Back here. Back to nothing." He sits up and faces away from me on the bed. He drops his elbows down to his knees and his head falls forward. I wait, my heart pounding, and finally he looks back up at me and goes on.

"I made it to the parking lot before I stopped. I'm not sure how long I stood there staring up at the stars wondering what the hell I was doing. Was I really going to walk away? But it was just as crazy to stay. Like you, earlier, my feelings were so intense, too intense and it frightened the hell out of me. I walked further into the parking lot but stopped when my phone rang. My parents' number flashed on the screen. I had told them all about you and everything that happened. My mom and I had talked a few times and she heard something in my voice that must have told her you were becoming more to me that just a friend and I wasn't just sticking around town to check on you because I was concerned; that I wasn't there just for Linc. She knew you were becoming something special to me. Abigail, you mean everything to me. When I heard my mom's voice, I broke and spilled my guts. I don't think I've felt more lost than I did in that moment. I was so confused and didn't understand my feelings. Why was I trying to walk away from you and at the same time, why couldn't I?" Nick keeps his head bowed.

I was so close to losing him and I didn't even know. Even though he's here, I'm scared. I find myself pulling my legs up and wrapping my arms around them and waiting.

"My mom, we've always been tight and had a close relationship. She's always said she can sense when something is wrong. I used to think it was just her being dramatic, but in that moment I'm sure she felt I needed her. The timing, she knew. We talked for a few minutes and she gave me the peace and the words I needed to run back to you," he says like he's in pain. "I couldn't get back to you soon enough, Abigail. I couldn't even wait for the elevator; I ran up five flights of stairs. I got there right as Blue and Jaycee were leaving." A small smile forms on his face.

"I'm sure I looked crazy, sweating and breathing hard, but they just grinned at me. Jaycee told me you woke up asked for me and it pissed me off that I wasn't there. Blue assured me you were fine and they had stayed with you until you fell back asleep. Even they knew." He gestures to his room with a swooping arc of his arm. "This is nothing. Means nothing. Nothing unless you're here with me to make it a home. To make a life with me. Everything in my life since you has changed for the better. It's like not believing in something or anything until you see it for yourself. Until you, I had no faith. I didn't love like this; therefore, I didn't believe it really existed. Not for me anyway."

He pries my arms away from body and pulls me to him until I'm straddling his lap naked. Still feeling scared at almost losing him, I wrap my arms around his neck and bury my face in his chest as his warm hands travel up and down my back. "I love you, Abigail. You're everything to me. I was so cold until you came into my life and I didn't even know it. You, my fire, are what keeps me warm." He pulls me closer. "I'd freeze to death without you." he says and stands. "Hold on." he warns and my legs wrap tight around his waist. "Let's take a shower and then go get our tree, okay?" he suggests as he starts walking towards what I assume is the bathroom "Darlin', do not freak out when you see the bathroom, okay?" he jokes, but his tone is laced with worry. I groan and drop my head back on his shoulders.

CHAPTER SEVEN

We enter the most spectacular bathroom with another amazing chandelier, sunken tub, and a shower that could fit at least ten people. It has the most elegant ivory colored double vanity. There's a separate makeup vanity with a royal blue cushioned wingback chair in front of it. I can't help but laugh a little when I see it and look back at him.

He sees what I'm looking at and actually blushes before he brings my laugh to a halt and has me slamming my lips down on his. "I had that made just for you. It's never been used and was installed just last night. I wanted it ready for you when you got here," he says bashfully.

We make our way into the shower and take our time washing each other before getting dressed and heading out to pick out our very first Christmas tree.

CHAPTER EIGHT

We climb into the truck's cab and I don't wait for him to ask, I scoot to the center and put on my seatbelt. I look back at the patio and see Buford and Elvis watching us.

"Can they go with us?" I ask, not taking my eyes off them.

Nick looks back at them and shakes his head. "If they're riding in the bed, we'll have no place to put the tree, darlin'." he replies and starts the truck. Ugh, good point. I slouch down in the seat and hear Nick chuckle. "Listen, when we get back, after we unload the tree, if there's still time, we'll take them for a ride, okay?" he tries to console me but it's not really working. He must notice that as he goes on. "And we'll bring them a treat?" That eases my guilt a little.

"Okay." I snuggle in closer to him as he turns the knob for the lights and shifts the truck into gear.

As the truck makes its way back up the path towards the main house, I take that time to look around. The sun is beginning to set and I see lights illuminated in the distance. I keep watching as we get closer. "What's down there?"

Nick follows my gaze and then takes the turn leading down to where the lights are. "I was going to show you around tomorrow but since we're here, I'll show you now."

A clearing comes into view with a circling of six wood cabins with covered porches and chimneys and a very nice large, red brick home sits off to the side. In the center of the cabins is a brick campfire pit with chairs and wooden benches around it and a few clay Chimineas spaced around the area. A light dusting of snow is covering everything and only two of the cabins have lights shining through the windows with smoke billowing from the chimney.

"The brick house is Red's, our ranch foreman and the cabins are where our ranch hands stay if they need a place. Some of the folks that work here are Lubbock natives and live close by so they make the drive in every day. Others who are just passing through or single, don't have a place, whatever reason, can stay in the cabins, free of a boarding fee, as long as they help with the property chores. My grandparents started the ranch doing it that way and when I take over, it'll stay that way. My mom, she believes anyone who helps with our land is family and treats them as such. My dad feels the same but still runs checks on everyone before they're allowed to bunk here. My mom spends most of her time home alone and my dad makes sure she's protected in every way he can. The house, it's different. Unique. It was built to protect the family who lives in it."

I'm not sure what that means but it gives me the chills. He makes it sound like the house is alive. I shake off the spooky feeling when Nick stops the truck and puts it in park as one of the cabin doors open.

A very tall, good-looking man walks out and down the steps towards the truck. Nick rolls down the window right as he reaches us.

"Hey, Huck," Nick says and the man reaches in and shakes his hand.

"Hey, Nick. What brings you down this way?" Only then does Huck notice I'm in the truck and when he sees me a huge grin spreads across his face. "Howdy, ma'am."

He's a ruggedly handsome man with short black hair, just long enough to style a little and a full beard. He has to be as big as Nick if not bigger.

"This your Abigail, Nick?" Huck asks.

"Yes, this is her." Nick says with a smile. "Abigail, this is Huck, as in Huckleberry."

Nick laughs when Huck reaches in the truck and punches him in the arm. "Ma'am, it's a family name. My momma didn't have a choice, but you can call me Huck."

I let out a small giggle and reach my hand over and shake his through the window. "Nice to meet you, Huck." I say before settling back into my seat. Huck nods and then leans against the truck door.

"Looks like we're going to get another round tonight. Everything okay if we do?" Nick asks, motioning to the dark sky.

"Yup. Pulled 'em all in and have them tucked in the barn and stables. Red's down at the barn now making sure they all have enough heat. He's making plans to stay in the loft tonight since one of the mares is expecting in a few days and seems agitated. It's probably just the weather; he thinks she has a few days yet. I might head down in a bit but Levi, well, he's not, let's just say, feeling too good so I'll wait and see. I told him to stay inside and call Darcy but he said he couldn't."

Nick and Huck share a look and shake their heads. "Hopefully he pulls his head out of ass soon." Nick says and Huck nods in agreement.

"News says the storm is moving in and the winds are going to kick up again around midnight. Says another eight to twelve inches could fall before morning. It's going to be a bad one. Where are y'all headed?" Huck voice turns to concern.

"Just down the road to the tree farm and then down to Main Street. Going to hit a couple of stores and pick up some Christmas decorations. Won't be gone long and if the storm moves in sooner, we'll head back."

Huck pushes off the truck and pats the side. "Then don't let me keep y'all. The sooner you get what you need and get back, the better."

"Alright then. We'll see you. Call me if you need to." Nick puts the truck back in gear and starts to make a turn that leads back up to the main road. Huck makes his way back to his cabin and with a final wave to us, goes inside.

"He was really nice." I'm happy to be finally meeting the people in Nick's life.

"Yes, he is. I've known him since kindergarten. Our parents went to school together. Most likely our grandparents too," Nick shares absently while steering the truck past the main house.

I turn and look as we go by. Holy shit. Now I see it for what it is. It's not a house, it's a mansion. "Um, Nick?" I choke out.

"Darlin', we had this talk. Stop," he says gruffly.

"Okay." is all I manage to squeak out as I keep staring at the beautiful brilliant white house with black shutters. Finally, I settle back in my seat and stare out the front window.

"Love you, Abigail." Nick says with tenderness in his voice and reaches over and takes my hand. He links our fingers before pulling them over to settle on his thigh.

"Love you too, Nick." I feel him let out a deep breath and his body relaxes. I need to stop overreacting. He loves me and I love him and we belong together.

We turn off the property and onto a main farm road that looks like nothing but a long road of pastures. It's probably going to be another long ride so I reach down and turn the stereo back on. Rather than the CD I turn on the radio. I need to learn the stations up here anyway. When the dial hits a country station I stop there and turn up the volume before snuggling back into Nick. We relax into one another as George Strait's *The Chair* sounds over the speakers.

Before too long I see white Christmas lights shining off on the side of the road where there's a line of vehicles. Nick pulls behind a truck and looks over at me. I start bouncing up and down on my seat.

"Let's go, honeysuckle." I squeal. He laughs and turns towards the door but before he can pull the door handle I grab his arm. I almost forgot to ask. "Nick, how tall is your ceiling?" I sure hope he knows, otherwise we may have to settle for a small tree or come back.

"In the living room, thirteen feet and the rest of the house are nine. Why?" he asks not yet understanding.

"Because that means we can get at least an eleven or twelve-foot tree. We have to leave room for the angel, or the star. I mean, do you have a preference on whether it's star or angel? But either way, it should be fine."

Nick shakes his head as he pulls the door handle opening the door. He cusses as he throws his leg out. "Walked right into that one. Didn't even see it coming," he mumbles which causes me to burst out laughing.

"Yes, you did and no, you didn't."

He takes my hand and pulls me down the gravel shoulder of the road to the entrance of the tree farm. After an hour of looking, we finally settle on a beautiful Douglas fir that stands almost eleven feet tall. Nick pays and then leaves me with the tree as he walks back to the truck and drives it up to the pickup point. One of the tree farm workers helps Nick load it up in the bed and tie it down while I wait inside the cab where it's warm.

A smile spreads across my face as we make our way into town. Nick pulls into the local Wal-Mart and we head straight for the Christmas decorations. After deciding on large bulb white lights we make our way to the ornaments. We ponder over the choices for what seems like hours, or I do anyway. Eventually we decide on red, blue and silver as the colors. I pick up some glass ornaments and some small wooden ornaments shaped as cowboy boots and hats, along with some Texas shaped one and Lone Star shaped ones. I find the coolest red paisley ribbon, like a western bandana that will be perfect for the bows. After loading up the basket with almost two dozen spools, a base for the tree along with a red tree skirt trimmed in white, we head down the final aisle. "Pick," I tell Nick, pointing to the section of tree toppers.

"No, darlin'. You pick." he says softly.

"Nick, it would mean more to me than you realize if you would pick the tree topper that goes on our first Christmas tree."

"Okay," he relents.

He looks back at the selection and after a couple of minutes, reaches for an angel. It has blonde hair and is wearing a white gown. The box says her wings and gown lights up. I smile and take it from him and put it in the cart before wrapping my arms around his waist.

"Thank you," I whisper as I go in for a kiss.

"You're welcome, darlin," he says softly against my lips.

It only takes a second before the kiss takes a turn. He grabs my face and kisses me passionately, right there in the middle of a Wal-Mart in West Texas and no one's batting an eye. I start laughing at the thought.

"Not one person is looking twice at us for making out."

Nick laughs. "Hell, we could probably do more than kiss and people would just walk around us. Want to try?" he jokes, taking my hand in one of his and pushing the cart with the other as we make our way through the store.

On the way, we pass the hardware department, and I ask to grab a couple of old metal wash tubs I see on one of the end caps. I'll figure out something to do with these. I love that he doesn't ask why and just loads everything up. When we finally make it to the pet section I pick up two rawhide bones fit for a t-rex and throw them in the cart along with some bacon looking treats and some with peanut butter centers. Nick laughs and shakes his head as he starts us towards the checkout.

In line and waiting for our turn at the checkout, I hear a woman voice with a super thick country drawl holler Nick's name. I turn to where the voice is coming from and see a woman sauntering towards us. She's tall and beautiful. Her deep auburn hair is swaying as she makes her way to us, smiling huge. She's wearing a pair of tight black hip hugging corduroys with a wide leather black belt. Her belt buckle, it's huge and shaped as a skull with two revolvers off the side and it catches and keeps my eyes for a few seconds. It's so cool. Her very snug low-cut black sweater is showing off her 'girls' and to finish off her vixen look, she's wearing thigh high black boots with four or five inch heels. She's freaking sexy as hell. She stops in front of us and leans in to hug Nick and give him a kiss on the cheek before looking over at me. She eyes me up and down and her huge smile gets wider as it shines across her face.

"This your Abigail, honey?" she asks Nick.

"Yes. This is her. Abigail, meet Starley Henderson. We went to school together." he tells me.

"We did more than go to school together, honey, we almost got married," she corrects him. Nick laughs as he rolls his eyes.

"Nice to meet you, Starley." I say, noticing the same humor in her eyes.

"Call me Star." she winks at me. "A lot of woman are going to be giving you hell for taking Nick off the market, sweetheart. I've heard Ashley and some of them are plotting to try and run you off so stay on your toes, okay?" She looks back at Nick. "You need to keep her close. Some of those nasty bitches don't know when enough is enough." she warns.

"I got this, Star. Don't." Nick says on a growl.

"Nick, should I be worried?" I ask, looking back and forth between him and Star.

"No, darlin', you got nothing to worry about. No one is going to bother you." He gives Star a stern look.

"Look, I'm just saying that rumors are flying that Ashley and her posse of stuck up bitches are pissed you went outside of town for a woman."

When Star says that I jerk my head back while thinking how ridiculous that is.

"Anyway, I have to go. I'm actually heading to your place. Heard Levi is feeling crabby, so taking him a little something." She holds up a box of condoms and a six pack of beer.

I giggle. "I don't know Levi but I'm guessing he'll feel better after those," I joke, pointing to the condoms.

Star laughs. "Oh, honey, only the beer is for Levi. The condoms are for Huck. I plan on timing it just right with this storm moving in so that I get stuck at his cabin all night."

I open my mouth in surprise before she winks at me again and walks off.

Nick grabs my hands and pulls me with him as the line moves closer to the cashier. I smile and look up at him. "I like her, Nick but y'all were almost married?" I ask.

"We were ten or eleven years old. I didn't ask, she told me I was going to marry her." he explains with a grin.

A bubble of laughter comes out of my mouth. "I can't believe you got away." I say and he gives me a look that says he almost didn't which makes me laugh again.

"We grew up together and like Huck, I've known her since grade school. She actually teaches in the elementary school we all went to. Most everyone around here goes way back. Levi, you'll meet him tomorrow. We didn't know him until high school. His family moved here the middle of our freshman year," he tells me as we keep moving with the line. "His mom died about a year ago, breast cancer. His dad's sorrow was just too deep for the loss of his wife. He died in his sleep a month after she passed. Sucks, Levi had to bury his mom and a month later, his dad. They were really good people. But Levi, he left town for a while. Went up to Montana and hid out at some lodge to clear his head but eventually came home. He put his family's home and land on the market and a few weeks ago. It's under contract for sale now so he wanted to move out of the house. Didn't want to be bothered with people coming in and out of his family home, judging it."

I nod in understanding. I can't imagine people going through my grandma or mom and dad's home picking it apart when I think it's perfect. We finally get to the register and Nick picks up the divider and places it in between the purchases from the person in front of us. We both start pulling things from the cart and laying them on the checkout belt as he goes on.

"So, he came by the main house to let us all know he was back and mentioned he was selling his folks' place, planned on checking into a motel in town until he figured out where to go. Levi's place connects along the back of ours. It's not big, just a few acres but it's a great piece of land. His parents always respected the land, took care of it taught Levi to respect it. My dad tried to talk him out of selling—but he said he needed the money. My mom insisted he come and stay in one of the cabins, and as long as he was helping out he wouldn't have to pay and could save up. The ranch hands that live out of town are gone until after the New Year so all but one cabin was empty. He took it and has been helping out around the ranch while we're working with a skeleton crew through the holidays. Though in winter, when it gets cold like this and we get a lot of snow, we herd the cattle into the barn and pen them, as many as possible anyway before the storm hits. Sometimes we can't get them all in so we make sure they have enough feed in those fields." He steps forward to where the cashier is scanning our items.

"Well, what about those you don't bring in? Won't they freeze or something?" I ask in concern.

"That could happen but doesn't. Farmers around here pay close attention to weather warnings and can start pulling their livestock days before any bad weather hits. No excuse for leaving 'em out to the elements but a lot of areas in the Midwest, the cold can be fatal for livestock. The wind can cause a lot of problems, cattle getting caught in snowdrifts trapping them, can't get to shelter or food and they starve. We get those drifts from time to time so we bring ours into the shelters during storms. Damage to fencing and them getting out, hurting themselves or not being able to get to their feeders are what I worry about. We do everything we can but sometimes, yeah, we lose some." He pulls me into a hug when he sees my sadness for the cows. He keeps me close as he swipes his credit card to pay for the decorations. "Sorry, didn't mean to upset you, Abigail. Darlin' you do realize we're a beef cattle ranch, right?" he whispers.

Yeah, okay. I have to come to terms with all this.

"Our cattle provide for us and we treat them as though they are a gift. We take care of them as best we can. Providing for them until they provide for us."

"I need to learn. I know. I'll be okay," I offer and then look at the total from the decorations. "Um, Nick, I can pay for some of those. I had planned on help—" I try to say but before I can finish my sentence, he slams his lips down on mine.

After silencing me with his kiss, he pulls back, giving me a look that tells me to shut up. I shudder before we both face the clerk who's grinning at us.

"Hey, Claire. How you doing?" Nick asks her.

She laughs. "Well, I'm doing alright, Nick. Not as good as her, but good. Thanks for asking. Sorry to see you out of the game but pleased as pie to see you happy. She's a beauty, baby," she says and tears off the receipt and hands it to Nick.

"Hi, I'm Claire." She reaches over to shake my hand. I accept and after a warm squeeze to my hand, she lets go.

"Nice to meet you too, Claire." I think I'm supposed to be jealous about meeting all these women I'm sure my man has done the nasty with but they're just so damn nice that I can't help but like them. No sooner has the thought crossed my mind then I hear a caddy whining voice call Nick's name from right behind us.

"I hate fucking Wal-Mart. The whole fucking town is always here. Jesus Christ, this is way I go to Target." Nick grumbles and I laugh as I turn around to find the queen of the bitch-face staring me down. "What do you want, Tina?" I laugh because she has a bitch-face, bitch-voice and her name is number one on the top ten list of bitch-girl list of names. At least Vogue says so.

"Stop it, Tina." a soft sweet voice says.

"Sorry, y'all." A pretty dark-haired woman with sparkling green says. "How are you, Nick?" she asks.

"I'm fine, Darcy. You?" Nick replies.

"Darcy, what the hell are you doing?" the bitch-face Tina asks before going on. "Your momma and daddy are going to be spitting mad that he actually brought her here."

"Abigail, I'd like you to meet Darcy Ramsey. Darcy, meet my Abigail." Nick introduces us, ignoring Tina.

"It's so nice to meet you, Abigail. I'm happy to see Nick finally in love and making plans." Darcy says while still smiling at us.

"Darcy?" Tina clips in a whining voice.

"Tina stop. Now, go on and wait for me at car. I'll be there in a second." Darcy orders softly but sternly. Tina huffs and walks off.

"Sorry about that. People in this town have a twisted notion about Nick and I. It's actually pretty gross since I've always looked at him like a brother." she says and fake shudders and gags and Nick laughs.

"So what's up with all this then?"

"Some folks think our two ranches should merge and make an even bigger monopoly on things around here but not Nick and I or his family. My family, sorry to say, have been pushing for Nick and I to get together to 'seal the deal' between the Cotton Princess and Cattle Prince as the town calls us." She rolls her eyes. "It was deemed our destiny for as long as I can remember by my parents," she sighs and shakes her head. "No matter how many times I've tried to tell them it's not like that, not in the least, they don't listen."

Nick finally speaks up. "Plus, Darcy here, she's been in love with Levi since he rolled into town fifteen years ago." She gasps and Nick chuckles. "Better hurry up and go get him Darcy." Nick says in a swift change to seriousness.

Darcy's eyes become wet with unshed tears. "I've tried, Nick. You know that but he still walked away. He left me," she says in the most heartbroken voice.

"But he's back, Darcy. He came back. Why do you think that is?" Nick finishes and that has hope flashing briefly in her eyes before fading just as fast.

"He only came back to settle things after his parents passed. He's selling his home and I don't know why other than he plans on leaving again. He loves that property. He's not staying and he's not back for me, Nick." she says, defeated.

"Sweetheart, if you believe that, you're crazy."

"What do you mean?" she asks.

"He could have done that from Montana, Darcy. He didn't have to come back and settle back in. He's looking for a place. Levi plans on staying. Just not at his parents' place. Sold it all. House, all the belongings, everything. Livestock and land too." Nick tells her while draping his arm across my shoulder and pulling me close.

My heart breaks for Darcy, but I feel a small amount of hope for her too.

He tilts his head before finishing. "As a matter of fact, he's back at the cabin now, sick. Star's dropping off some stuff to help with his ailment, hoping to help him feel better." Nick baits her.

"What? He's sick?" she replies, frantic, but then quickly pulls herself together a little. "That's nice of her. I'm sure he'll appreciate it." she says before looking away.

Nick chuckles, and then winks at me. "After Star drops it off, she plans on getting stranded over at Huck's. We both know Star has been in love with Huck since we were all in middle school and she's tired of waiting. She's going after her man. You should too," he says before leaning down and giving her a kiss on the cheek. "We'll talk soon."

I stop and turn back to Darcy. "Would you like to get together for lunch one day? Maybe you can show me around? I'd love to make some friends around here," I ask shyly, but realizing these people are important to Nick, and therefore, important to me.

74

"I'd love that. I'll call Nick later and get your number or he can just give you mine and you call me when you have time." she says with a huge smile.

We all jolt in surprise when we hear Claire holler from a few aisles over. "Count me in! And Star too. We'll do a girls day," she calls out and goes back at waiting on her customer who looks to be just as surprised as us.

"You got it, Claire," Darcy semi-hollers back and waves. "Alright. Well I'll see y'all later. Now I have to go listen to Tina whine the entire ride back at her house." she frowns and gives us a small wave as she walks away.

"Again, I like her, Nick. I like them all," I say to him while pulling him close.

"That's good darlin'." He tips his head down for a quick kiss before leading us out to the truck.

CHAPTER NINE

After loading up our Christmas decorations from our trip to Wal-Mart, we make our way back through town and Nick stops at a local diner called *Zink's*.

"This place has the best chicken fried steak. You up for grabbing dinner here?" he asks.

"I'd love that," I reply, only now realizing I'm starving.

"Let's go." he says and opens the truck door as I unfasten my seatbelt and slide out the driver's door. Nick grabs my hand we walk towards the entrance of the small diner. When he pushes the door open, a cowbell clanks loudly and I smile. Inside, there's red vinyl covered booths and small four seater tables all around. We pass the hostess stand which is empty and Nick pulls me down the roll of booths that are lined up by the front window facing Main Street. He picks one towards the end of the row and we sit down. Only one other booth is occupied by a couple of older gentlemen in blue jean overalls and dingy baseball caps. I can hear them talking about the weather and it makes me smile.

As soon as I take off my coat and tuck it beside me on the booth a woman's voice with a deep raspy southern drawl calls out. "Hey y'all. What can I get you to drink?"

When I look up, I instantly smile at the older, bleached blonde waitress with her hair in a beehive style, chewing gum. She's holding a pad in one hand and a pencil in the other.

"Um, what do you have?" I ask with a smile.

She smiles back and tucks her pencil behind her ear. "Well, baby doll, we got pretty much everything but Nick here, he favors our sweet tea and coffee. So do I." she says while placing her hands on her hips and waiting.

"Sweet tea it is then, ma'am." I say and look over at Nick who's grinning.

"Alright, baby doll, but my name is Bubbles. I appreciate the respect but I much prefer Bubbles." she says.

She walks away without asking Nick what he wants.

"Yes, ma'am, I mean Bubbles." I say to her retreating back.

For an older woman, she still has a good swing to her hips. A grin spreads across my face when I take in the two older men following her sassy swinging hips with their eyes as she retreats behind counter to get our drinks. Nick laughs and I look back.

"Is this for real?" I ask and he laughs louder.

"Yup. You likin' it?" he asks as he reaches over and pulls my hands across the table and holds them in his.

"I love it, honeysuckle." I reply, staring into his eyes and thinking how perfect my name for him is.

After Bubbles brings our drinks and takes our orders, Nick begins telling me more about the ranch. This upcoming year is their one-hundred-year anniversary and his mom is planning a huge barn dance.

Bubbles comes back a little while later and drops a plate in front of each of us. Both plates are oversized and hold an ear of corn, mashed potatoes, chicken fried steak smothered in cream gravy and cornbread. The steak is so big the ends are almost hanging off the plate. While wondering how I'll ever be able to eat all of this, Bubbles bring back another plate with a few rolls. "Wasn't sure which one you'd like. Brought both. Y'all need anything else?" Bubbles asks.

"No, looks good. Thank you, Bubbles." Nick says and I stare at my plate.

Good Lord. I'm going to die when my stomach explodes.

Trying to act like I'm unintimidated by the size of my meal, I dig in. Between bites Nick and I talk.

He tells me about a couple of bands that will take the stage at the celebration. One being southern rock and the other pure country. It sounds really exciting and I'm looking forward to being around for it. I can't wait to meet his parents. The way he talks about them, they sound amazing. He tells me we'll go up in the morning for breakfast and I can meet them, Levi, Red and some of the other hands that will be making their way in if the roads are okay to travel on after tonight's expected snowstorm.

As if on cue, I glance out the window and a few flurries are starting to fall. The flurries glistening in the light of the moon look beautiful. Bubbles walks back over with a container and the check and while Nick grabs money from his pocket and gives it to her, I peek in the container. I thought I was full but this, *this* I'll make room for. It's a huge slice of strawberry pie with tons of whip cream.

"Thank you, Bubbles." I say and she winks and walks off as Nick and I grab our coats and hats and put them on as we make our way out of the diner.

Traveling back to the ranch, the snow starts coming down but still not too bad. Nick makes the turn off to the cabin and I get excited about being stuck with him in the cabin during the storm, like Darcy and Star, all us girls have the same fantasy of being trapped one way or another with our hot alpha men for a few days while their only goal is to please their woman. I want to be that woman tonight, tomorrow night and if possible the next night. Yes, most likely all those nights and more.

Pulling up in front of the cabin, Buford and Elvis are waiting for us and I can't wait to give them their treats. Nick gets out of the truck walks around, opening the passenger side door and starts loading up his hands with the Wal-Mart bags while I grab my container of strawberry pie.

"Darlin', let's get in and I'll call Huck and Levi or Red to help me pull this tree in the house before it gets much worse." Nick says as he pulls the metal tubs from the truck and hands them to me. "These are a little small to bathe the dogs in, Abigail." He grins and I laugh because they'd be more like a water bowl for them.

"No, I think I'm going to use them as pots for poinsettias and put them on the front porch," I answer, looking at the tubs and pondering.

"That would be real nice. Let's go." Nick says when the snow starts to fall heavier. We walk up the steps where Elvis and Buford are waiting, their tails thumping lazily. Nick opens the door and steps back so I can walk in first with Elvis and Buford following him in. I keep going but stop when I notice both dogs halt and wait by the door. I watch as Nick puts all the bags down and walks back to Elvis and Buford. They're sitting perfectly still except for their panting and tails thumping. Setting the tubs down, I keep my eyes on them. Nick pulls an old towel from a hamper next to the door and squat down in front of them.

He leans towards Elvis. "Ladies first," he reminds her and Elvis lifts her left paw and Nick wipes it with the towel. "You're all good, girl. Go on." Elvis trots over a few feet and sits down. I stare and smile as he repeats the entire process with Buford. The smile on my face stays in place as I set the tubs down and put my pie in the refrigerator.

"That's impressive, Nick." I turn around in time to meet Nick as he walks over pulls me into a hug.

"Don't think you want mud and snow tracked in and up on the bed covers since you're letting them up there with you." He leans in and kisses me. I hear two different groans and then thumps so I pull back from Nick and look over to see Elvis is asleep and Buford is looking bored. I can't help but laugh.

"Hang on, darlin'. Going to give Huck a call," he tells me. He starts throwing some logs into the fireplace along with some kindling before lighting it. I take this time to look around the front of the house. It's open with a huge kitchen and breakfast counter opening into a family style room where the fireplace is. The fire is burning and small orange flames begin to take over the logs and it's hypnotizing. Nick walks into the kitchen while on the phone talking and grabs two bottles of water from the fridge. He has his phone to his ear when he looks up and sees me watching him and he winks at me, causing me to blush. He gestures at me to grab the water so I walk over and take it before returning to the fireplace.

I once again study the room as the warmth from the fire fills it. A mixture of small boulders and jagged brick are being used for the foundation, hearth and to line the interior smoke chamber. The mantel has an old log braced across the smaller logs replicating the build of the log cabin. The style reminds me of Lincoln logs and how I'd watch my brothers build things with them. The firebox is black and large and next to it is a hollow enclave in the brick and stone where some logs are stored.

As my eyes travel around the room, I see the same style above the arched doorways. The ceiling in the family room itself is exposed logs but everywhere else looks like regular ceilings, only taller. A series of arch topped windows run along the entire back wall and I can see the back porch illuminated by the light with snow softly and silently drifting down. I turn to the kitchen but stop when I see Nick staring at me and smiling sweetly.

"Do you like it, fire?" he asks.

"I love it, Nick." Glancing at the kitchen, I see all the appliances are stainless steel. The flooring is a deep rich wood. I run my hands along the black granite counter tops and feel their smoothness. I shyly smile at Nick as I take a deep breath.

"It's beautiful. You have a beautiful home Nick," I say almost in a whisper.

"It's our home, Abigail. Ours. For now. After we get married and have kids, I'll build us a bigger house. I'll let you design it. It'll be ours." He leans in and kisses me. Nick lifts me by my butt and I wrap my legs around his waist as he makes his way back into the kitchen and sets me on the counter. He kisses me as his hands start for my sweater. He pulls it up and off just as his phone starts ringing. "Shit. The tree. I called Huck. He's coming up but I told him to call on his way up to let me know if Levi was coming too," he says and stands back pulling his phone from his pocket. "What?" he growls into the phone.

"Dude, what the hell? You called me!" Hearing the muffled irritated voice makes me laugh and I jump off the counter and pull my sweater back on. Walking into the dining area, six tan leather back chairs are tucked neatly underneath a long varnished oak table. I brace my hands against the top of one and stare out the window. The snow seems to be slowing again. Maybe the storm isn't going to be as bad as the forecast predicted. Arms come around my waist and Nick's warm breath blows against my neck.

"They'll be here in about fifteen minutes," he tells me. "Darcy and Star are with them." He chuckles as he kisses my neck and his warm tongue tastes me. I shiver but smile knowing Darcy took the bait and went to Levi, but let out a moan when I feel his tongue go up behind my ear. I push back against him when his hands tighten around my waist and he pushes back into me and I feel how hard he is which causes another moan to leave my lips.

"Fuck, darlin'. We need to stop," he says while pushing against me again.

"Okay. Show me the rest of the place," I say while turning in his arms and pressing my lips to his. I hear a pained groan as he pulls back and stares down in my eyes before taking my hand and starting towards the hallway across from the one that leads to his or our bedroom.

"Our bedroom and bathroom are the only rooms off that side except for a storage closet and a coat closet in the hallway," he points towards where our bedroom is. "This way is two guest bedrooms, my office and a half bath. Each bedroom is an ensuite but with very small bathrooms." He pulls me down the hallway and opens the first door and I glance in and see a queen size bed with leathered back headboard, a dark wood dresser with matching nightstands. The lamps on either side are brass with small tan lampshades. He pulls me in further and I see, like he said, a small bathroom with a small dark wood stand alone vanity with curved legs. The shower is all glass and there's a window out the side with plantation shutters. He pulls me back out and closes the door as he makes his way down the hall to the next door and opens it. "My office," he says and pulls me in. I glance around to a very untidy desk and my eyebrows scrunch together as I look at him. "Believe it or not, I know where everything is. It's organized chaos," he says in defense. There's a laptop sitting open on the desk along with a lamp. Two rather large chairs covered in a rawhide pattern sit across from his cherry wood desk and some hunting trophy heads are mounted. Frames along the wall catch my attention and I realize this is the only room I've seen with any personal touches. I make a note to come look at them later. The same style of windows that are in the family room run along his office wall. I can see the back patio so it must run the entire length of the cabin.

"How big is this place, Nick?" I ask absently as he pulls me back out of the room and down to the next door.

"It's 3,800 square feet," he replies as he opens the third door and shows me the half bath with ivory pedestal sink painted in a deep rich hunter green and trimmed in white. There's a smaller window on the back wall with the same plantation shutters as the first room. He pulls me back out and then walks a few steps to the last door in the hallway on the opposite side of the other room and opens the door. All the door handles are an antique bronze color with levers rather than knobs. It's the small touches that are making this cabin so beautiful. As Nick opens the door I intake swiftly. It's beautiful.

The bed is huge, like Nick's. It's covered in thick white frilly covers with no headboard. The end tables are white with crystal lamps sitting on them with delicate white lamp shades. There's a simple wooden chair, worn but painted white sitting across from the bed and beside that is an oval mirror with brass framing hanging from the wall. A freestanding light oak wood wardrobe sits across from the back wall and like the family room and office, is mostly windows. But these are divided into eight sections with lacy white sheer curtains dividing each panel. "Oh, wow, Nick. This is breathtaking." I say as I walk into the bathroom sitting off to the side. There's a double slipper claw foot tub with ceiling mounted shower ring. It's got tub mounted brass fixtures with a gooseneck faucet and hand shower. I'm going to have to use this. Better yet, Nick and I are going to have to use this. We both have the same look so I know he's thinking what I'm thinking. This beautiful tub is going to be seeing some action. I rise up on my tiptoes and kiss him with all I have. His hands go to my ass where he pulls me to him and I can feel he's still hard. I start kissing him deeper but freeze when I sense we're being watched.

I turn and see Buford and Elvis there, sitting on their haunches, staring at us. "Oh, my God, Nick, stop." I squeak and start squirming out of his arms.

"They don't know, darlin'," he says his voice laced with humor.

"Oh, they know, Nick. Look at how they're looking at us." I reply as there's a knock on the front door.

"Going to let them in," he says with laughter still in his voice.

I try to act nonchalant and slip my hands into my back pockets and look around but really I'm watching Buford and Elvis out of the corner of my eye. They haven't moved so look out the window, ignoring their stares while to convince myself they have no idea what was going on. When I turn around, both Buford and Elvis are still sitting, resting on their haunches waiting for me to explain. It's the most alert I've seen Elvis. "It's not what you think. You're worried your daddy's new girl is a floozy. I'm not," I reassure them and let out a nervous cough to clear my throat. I watch as both of them raise their doggy eyebrows at me as to say, oh really?

"Really." I say and watch their heads tilt to the side. *Kill me now.*

"Let's go." I demand weakly. "I'll give you both a treat if you promise we never speak of this again." When neither moves, I walk around them and start for the door, stopping when they each softly bark at my back. Both of them now have sad eyes.

"Come here. It's fine. You'll see. We'll all be good together. Happy. Let's get those treats for y'all." I coax them.

My heart warms with they come to me one on either side and place their heads under my palms. After a quick head rub we make our way out of the room and down the hall and I and search the bags for their treats.

When I find them and open the bag, I look down and both of them are sitting, waiting expectantly. I laugh as Buford lifts his paw and I lean down and shake it. "Good boy, Buford. Here," I give him two treats which he takes in his mouth and walks off. Elvis walks up next and lifts her paw but not for a shake but a high five. That makes me laugh too. She's a little show-off. "That's a good girl," I say and high-five her before handing her two treats which she takes and goes to lay next to Buford by the fireplace. I close the bag and brush my hands off on my jeans and stand up and let out a squeal when I see Star and Darcy standing behind me having watched the entire thing. Their faces bright as they smile warmly at me.

We all go and stand next to fireplace but before we can speak the front door opens and the tip of our tree comes through the threshold with a hot looking guy leading the way and directing them. He's got a black wool pinched front cowboy hat drawn down deep on his head. He's looking around to make sure they won't hit anything but when his eyes reach me, they stop. He smirks, forgets what he is doing and walks over to me.

Mother of God, he's hot. He has jet black hair that hangs down just past his shoulders and deep blue eyes. He looks like he has a touch of American Indian in him. Holy hot damn. I stand frozen as he makes his way to me, my eyes never leaving his. I think I'm drooling and if I'm not, I should be.

"Hi, there. You must be Abigail." He reaches out and takes my hand. I haven't answered and I'm still frozen in my place. I can hear Darcy and Star giggling as I stare at his beautiful smile.

I only slightly come of my lust slumber when I hear Nick yell. "Hey, Levi, want to help us out here?"

"Yeah, sure. I'll be right there." Levi answers without looking away from me and still holding my hand. I finally shake off all impure thoughts and laugh when I hear Nick cuss.

"Hey, asshole, you better not be touching my girl." The tree is making its way inside with Huck holding it up by the rope tied around the middle. Levi stands back, my hand in his as he throws his arm around my shoulder, watching and waiting until Nick walks through the door holding the end of the tree. When Nick's eyes make it to us and he sees Levi holding my hand and his arm around me, he promptly drops the tree which causes Huck to cuss and drop the middle. When Nick starts at us, Levi starts laughing and backs away, holding up his hands to placate Nick.

"Look, lover boy. Not touching anymore," Levi says and Huck laughs. "You pulled me out in the cold. I was just keeping warm." Levi jokes, which causes Nick to lunge for him. Levi dodges Nick and then hurdles himself over the back of the couch and grabs Darcy, pulling her in front of him for protection.

Everyone in the room, including Nick, starts laughing.

"Use your own woman to keep you warm." Nick says as he pulls me to him. I see something flash in both Darcy and Levi's eyes before he gently releases her from his arms.

When she starts to back away from him, clearly disappointed, Levi pulls her back and wraps his arms around her waist. She rests her hands on his chest looking down but he leans down and whispers in her ear. Everyone has gone quiet. Maybe this is the moment everyone has been waiting for.

Over the crackling of the fire, Levi says, "Are you still my woman, baby?" Her nails dig into his chest at his words. I can see her lips move. I don't need sound to hear her voice when she says, "Always." With that he leans in and kisses her. Like really kisses her.

CHAPTER TEN

I guess we should all look away and give Levi and Darcy privacy but like me, none of us do. We stand and stare as she wraps her arms around his neck and pulls him closer. He angles his head to kiss her deeper when she finally reaches up and pulls off his cowboy hat and holds it in her hands against his back. When she does that, he groans and wraps his hands around her back pulling her so close and tight that it looks like it might even hurt, but Darcy doesn't complain. She just kisses him harder. When they part, Darcy has tears pouring down her cheeks. Levi tries wiping them with his thumbs put they're just falling too fast. He cups her cheeks and pulls her face to his.

"Enough, baby," he growls. "I'm talking to him. You're not going back. From this moment on, we become us. You're not leaving and I'm not leaving," he says in a deadly serious tone. Darcy nods frantically and then wraps him up tight.

Nick pulls me close and holds me. Huck is holding Star and she has tears running down her face. I didn't even see him walk to her. I was so enthralled in what was happening with Levi and Darcy; I didn't even notice I was crying too. The emotion between them being so strong it took us all over. Levi and Nick share a nod and then their eyes go to Huck and the same private message is passed before he gives a nod.

Okay, something is clearly about to go down. I'll have to talk to Nick about it later. About the same time as everyone else, I look back at the open front door and see the tree still lying in the threshold.

Nick kisses my cheek and releases me as he walks back at the tree. "Dude, where's the tree's base and where do you want it?" Huck asks. Oh crap, I didn't even think of that. I start rummaging through the Wal-Mart bags until I find the base. Star and Darcy flank me and all three of us glance around the room; stopping at the same spot. Along the back wall of window, the center window being the largest, I point to that spot and then look at Star and Darcy for confirmation. When Star gives me a thumbs up I turn to Darcy who looks at me with a shaky smile. She nods and confirms she likes the spot too. I can't help it, I reach over and pull her into a hug and then feel Star come up and join our huddle.

After getting the tree stand in place near the window, the guys get the tree secured. I turn and offer everyone a drink but they politely decline, promising to see us at breakfast. The girls say goodbye with hugs and the guys with shoulder bumps. After watching them all jump into a huge truck, Nick closes the door and turns back at me. We both look at the tree and then walk over to the table and start going through the bags pulling out decorations and lights. Nick tells me he'll be back and leaves for a few moments before coming back with a step ladder.

CHAPTER ELEVEN

I stand back, laughing my butt off, as I watch Nick spend almost two hours fussing and cussing while fighting with the strings of lights and almost knocking over the tree a few times when he leaned too far into it on the ladder. Finally, he gets them all on and working. I giggle loudly when he lets out a breath of relief and drops his head.

"That's much harder than it looks. Going to buy my dad a beer, no two, next time we're out to thank him for not tossing the Christmas trees out each year. I was so close to losing it." he says.

We pull out the ornaments and hooks and once we fasten the hooks to the bulbs we start hanging them. Nick concentrates towards the top while I hang towards the middle and bottom. Once we get all the ornaments hung, I walk over and pull out the ribbon and start making bows while handing them off to Nick to tie them on the branches. When everything is in place, we stand back and take it all in.

"The angel," I blurt out in panic and rush back over to the bags and pull it out and hand it to Nick, but he doesn't take it. Instead he pulls the ladder over and sets it next to the tree, and then reaches out for my hand. When I take it, he pulls me over, helps me up and then steps up behind me. I get in position and Nick hands me the angel and I slide it in place while he holds me steady. I reach down and find the plug on the lights and plug the angel in and watch it light up. Nick helps me step down and then we look at the tree. He wraps his arms around my waist as he leans his mouth against my ear. "I picked that angel because it looks just like you." he says with love.

This is a huge step. An important step. This will define every Christmas to follow. I put my hands on Nick's arms and squeeze. He lets go and I turn so I can pull him into a hug.

"It's beautiful, Abigail. Beautiful just like you," he says as he leads me over to the couch to sit down. I snuggle up beside him and as I glance between the hypnotizing fire and Christmas lights, suddenly my eyes start drooping.

"Come on, fire." Nick stands and pulls me with him. "Let's get to bed." He leads me down the hallway to the bedroom.

CHAPTER TWELVE

Once in the bedroom, I start for my suitcases but Nick stops me and pulls me behind him as he walks to his dresser and grabs an old t-shirt. "Just wear one of my shirts. You can unpack tomorrow. Go on and do what you need to do. I need to put up the ladder and let Buford and Elvis out one last time. Crawl into bed and stay warm. I'll join you soon," he says and leans down and gives me a soft peck on the lips before walking out the door. I drowsily walk into the beautiful bathroom and start pulling off my clothes and placing them in his hamper. Wow, that's a huge step. I stand and stare at our mixed clothes before turning back to the basin while pulling Nick's shirt over my head. I take in his scent for a few seconds, loving it. I don't know whether it's his detergent or him, but it just does something to me. It's the best thing to ever fill my senses. Deciding I don't want the hassle of going through my carry-on for my toiletries, I grab Nick's toothbrush and toothpaste and brush my teeth before using his brush to brush out my hair. After I'm done I put everything back in its place and wipe down the counter. Leaving the bathroom, I run into a hard chest. I smile at Nick as he leans down and kisses me. His hands go to the sides of my face where he lets his finger run through my hair.

"Darlin', you used my stuff," he says against my lips. It's not a question. "I love that you used my shit," he goes on as he pulls me into him. "Anyone else did that; I'd probably kick their ass. You fuck me, but I love that you used my things. We're one," he whispers against my ear causing me to shiver.

His eyes travel my face and he brings his fingers up and begins to trace my lips and cheeks. "Almost let you go. Fucking stupid. I shouldn't have fucked around and waited. Should have gone down there and brought you back even if you fought me kicking and screaming," he says on a long blink, then drops his head and lets out a pained sigh. "I shouldn't have waited. I shouldn't have given up," he whispers, his eyes drawing together like he's in pain.

Given up? My heartbeat and breath come to a halt.

"Darlin', we are what we are now. Not going to let anything change that again but I need to tell you something. I need you to understand though...fuck," he snaps and steps back. He looks out the windows before continuing. "I wanted to do this tomorrow or never but I have to." He takes a deep breath. "Abigail, I thought...darlin', I thought you didn't want me and it fucking hurt. It hurt badly. I needed to stop the pain. I tried drowning myself in the ranch, but nothing worked. I reached for the bottle, Abigail. I was just trying to drink away some of the pain. I never meant for anything else to happen," he confesses and frowns at me. "I went out. I was drinking. I was talking about you. It was all about you. I wanted the pain to stop." his voice trails off as he whispers. "I'm sorry," his voice is strained, his expression reminding me of someone having their heart ripped out.

His hands come back to my face and he begins tracing my lips again. I'm letting his words sink in and when he feels me start to react, suddenly one of his hands goes into my hair and the other goes to my neck. I try to put a little distance between us, but his grip on both tighten. He's scared I'm going to run away and he should be. Inside my heart begins to beat again but it takes on the rhythm of a bass drum. My stomach is flipping and I suddenly feel sick. I try to control my breathing but it becomes heavy and I feel a burn in my nose and eyes. I know what he's saying and it feels like someone just stabbed me in my heart. Too far? He needed to stop the pain? He sees that I know and tears drop from my eyes. We had such a beautiful day. How in a moment did it all change? My legs grow weak as I stare in his eyes and shake my head rejecting his words. Begging for it not to be what I think it is, but when his hands grip me tighter and he pulls me in closer, I know. I look down as a silent sob jerks my body before looking back up at him and see his eyes are glassy too.

"You slept with someone?" I whimper out.

With unshed tears he apologizes again. "I'm sorry. I love you."

I don't even know I'm going to do it. It just happens. I jerk out of his grasp and slap him. His head doesn't even move. He doesn't reach to soothe his own pain. He lowers his head for a few moments before he looks back up at me, his face full of shame and sorrow. I stare at my hand when I feel the sting on my palm. He reaches out, takes it and looks at the redness as guilt takes over his face, but I jerk back from him. I'm grateful for a moment of distraction away from the pain in my heart. I lose it and start hitting his chest. I've never been a violent person but I'm no pushover either. I've never hit anyone in my life. Not even my brothers but right now I can't stop.

Nick grabs my wrists and pulls them behind me to stop me from hitting him. "I'm sorry. I'm sorry. I love you. No, darlin'. I love you. Stop. You're hurting yourself."

The scream that leaves my throat breaks even my heart. "Why? Why didn't you tell me before I came here? Changed everything in my life for you?" I sob through a scream. "I was hurting too. I'm hurting now! Let me go! I'm leaving. I'm going home and finding someone to fuck the pain out of me," I scream and try pulling away from him, but his grip tightens.

"Fuck! No you're not, Abigail," he bellows but quickly calms himself and his voice turns pleading. "Please don't say that. You're not leaving me, Abigail. I won't let you."

"Yes, I am," I scream.

"Goddammit! Stop! I will kill anyone who touches you, Abigail," he warns in a deadly hiss. "I can't live without you. Stop," he growls.

Pain slices through my throat when I scream at the top of my lungs. "Oh, you'll be just fine without me!" I yell while still fighting his hold. "So who was it? Darcy? Star? Are they laughing at me right now? Hmmmm? Are you all having a great laugh at my expense?" My throat burns with every word and my voice is cracking. Finally, my voice disappears as I start coughing and pull away from him.

"Darlin', please. Stop." he pleads and draws me back into his arms tight. "I'm sorry. I was so fucked up and hurt. You hadn't called and I thought..." he whispers against my ear.

I rip myself from his arms and point at him. "Don't you dare blame me," I spit out. My voice is raspy and I'm still coughing as I jerk back.

We both stop when we hear a commotion near the entrance. The door to the cabin is open and standing there is an older version of Nick and a beautiful brunette with brown eyes just like Nick's and they both have alarmed looks on their faces.

"Nick, what the hell is going on?" the man asks as he stands aside and lets Buford and Elvis inside. The woman leans down and grabs the towel from the hamper and hastily wipes their feet while glancing back and forth between the dogs, Nick and I. Nick doesn't speak. He just stares at me. His chest is rising and falling with his labored breathing. All I can think is I can't stay, but how can I leave? I'm pulled from my thoughts when the man starts towards Nick. Nick sucks in a breath before facing the man.

"Dad, Abigail and I are working through something," he explains and looks at me. His eyes plead for something, anything. I narrow my stare at him as my pain begins turning to extreme anger. I take deep breaths to calm down but I can't stop the hitching no matter how hard I try. "We were just driving down to the stable to check on Shelly. Saw that the dogs were out. They were sitting in front of your place crying. Thought someone was hurt," Nick's dad explains. "Abigail, do you need to come up to the main house tonight?" he asks cautiously.

I hear Nick growl before he barks out, "No!"

"Nick! Pull it together," his dad barks back as him.

Nick runs his hands through his hair in obvious frustration. "Abigail, this is Ronan and China Callaghan, my parents. If you want to go with them, I understand. I won't stop you, but I'm begging you not too," he groans.

Something in my heart is telling me to stay. I've never felt so conflicted in my entire life. I promised my dad that this wasn't move wasn't going to be a mistake. That damn promise is what's going to keep me from leaving tonight but I won't hang around and be mistreated

CHAPTER THIRTEEN

I hang my head for a few moments, trying to gather myself. I start to speak but nothing comes out. My scream must have damaged vocal chords. Hearing movement, I glance at Nick in the kitchen filling a glass with water, bringing it over to me. With my shaky hand I accept it and take a few sips. It's soothing the burn so I take a few more. When I drain the glass, Nick is there to take it from me and set it on the table by the couch.

I try to smile at his parents. "I'll be fine, I'm so sorry we had to meet this way. That you saw me this way," I whisper, my voice hoarse.

"It's my fault. All my fault," Nick says to me as he walks carefully toward me. Because he's worried I'm going to lash out or run, he keeps a few feet between us. I can see his heart breaking at the fear of losing me "We're taking the dogs with us tonight. Come get them tomorrow or the next day. They'll be okay. Y'all work through what you need to do." Nick's dad tells us.

A tiny jerk leaves my body at the sound of the door closing and then I turn on Nick.

God, how did it turn so bad, so fast?

CHAPTER FOURTEEN

"Nick, I need to think. I need time. I don't think I can do this. Maybe we weren't meant to be. Maybe we're trying to push something that just doesn't fit. I hurt you. You hurt me." My voice is a whisper of doubt and confusion.

"We are not a mistake, Abigail. We just need to be together. Please." He starts to plead.

"Nick, you need to give me time I think. I should go home for a few days." I turn and look out the window.

"I want to explain..."

"NO!" My voice cracks in strain so I whisper, "You slept with someone else. There is no explanation. There is nothing you can say that will ever make that okay. Never." I walk over and stand in front of the Christmas tree. I think back to Nick fighting with the string of lights and how he picked the angel because it looks like me. Who is the real Nick? The loving, sweet man from our time together? Or is Nick the one he told me about earlier? The one who doesn't want a wife and family. Maybe that's the real Nick. Duty-bound by our circumstances. Obligated because he saved my life.

"Darlin, okay, please. I'll give you space here. Please don't leave. I'll sleep on the couch or in one of the cabins. You can go to my parents, but please don't leave me again. Please. I'm begging you, Abigail."

"This is your home. I'll go to the cabin." I move down the hallway to the bedroom and begin gathering my bags.

"Abigail, stop it." he growls. "I'm going to the cabin. I don't want to. I want to stay here, with you, but if this is what you need I'll give it you. Just don't leave. I'll call you in the morning. If you need anything before then, just call me."

Nick walks over and stares into my eyes for a moment before reaching out for me. I quickly take a step back avoiding his touch. He bows his head and his shoulders slump as he turns and walks out. I stand and listen as the front door closes and he starts his truck. I listen until I can't hear his truck anymore and then I rush to the phone and call Jaycee.

For the next two hours, Jaycee tries to comfort me. She repeatedly tells me she wants to come to Lubbock, but I beg her not to. I crave her support but I know I must do this on my own. I need to trust and believe in myself enough to figure this out. Plus, I know my dad and brothers will come get me without giving me a choice or even a discussion if they knew the truth.

"Jaycee, I'll be okay. You went through much worse than this." My voice is still hoarse from the force of my scream.

"Sissy, I had everyone around me," she reminds me softly.

"Listen, I'll be fine. I'm going to get some sleep. I'll call you in the morning, okay?" My lips begin to tremble and I hold back my whimpers at breaking our connection.

I really do need her. With Nick gone and not being able to turn and have Jaycee within reaching distance, I feel like I just might break.

"Jaycee, please keep this just between us. I've been here less than twenty-four hours. I need time to see if I can figure out what's going to happen. Please don't tell Mom and Dad or our brothers."

"But..." she begins to protest.

"Jaycee, please?"

"Okay. But you better call me in the morning. Promise?"

"I promise and I love you."

"I love you too," she whispers.

I wait a moment, but then hang up. I know Jaycee. She'll wait for me to hang up first in case I call out to her. My big sister, her heart.

Most of the night I lie awake; my thoughts of pain disguised as anger. My head wants me to call my dad and have him come up here and get me out, never looking back. My heart wants my head to shut up because it wants Nick. No, my heart doesn't just want Nick, it belongs to Nick.

Jaycee finds her strength in her kindness. Her strength resonates from her heart. My sister is as pure as snow. Some would think she'd be weak but she's the opposite. Sweet Jaycee is stronger than all the McGinty's put together. The two McGinty sisters, we look nothing alike. Both of us favoring our mom's, I guess. On the inside though I always thought Jaycee was so much stronger than me. Her ability to forgive and see the good over the bad was so much different than how I am or so I thought. I now know how she's able to forgive so easy and where her strength comes from. She loves unconditionally. From the deepest depth of her heart and soul, she loves. I think I get it now. My love for Nick outweighs what he did. Still, my feelings are too raw to even talk about forgiving him. I lie in bed, Nick's bed, our bed, and toss and turn all night. I'm thankful when gold starts streaming across sky.

Throughout the day, I walk around like a zombie. I sit around looking at the Christmas tree and wander through the house. I walk into Nick's office and stop in front of the photos on the wall, gazing at ones of him with his parents. There's several of him with calves and cows holding a blue ribbon. Some he's just a little boy, an adorable little boy. Others look like they could be as rescent as yesterday and he looks so handsome. There are aerial shots of the farm and I'm in awe at the amount of cattle shown.

I make my way along the side wall. There's a few hunting trophies, some golf clubs leaning against the wall and shelves filled with sports memorable. I sit down in one of the chairs facing Nick's desk and close my eyes and start crying. I want to stay but wouldn't that make me a fool? Something brushes against my legs, and I let out a stunned and frightened cry; jumping up. I quickly calm when I see its Buford and Elvis standing in front to me. I know I closed the office door, but regardless, there they are.

I turn around, even through my hurt I wish to see Nick standing there, only he's not and that makes me cry more. He must have known I needed them though. I drop down on the floor and both of them rest their heads in my lap and comfort me through more tears. Finally, I calm enough to give them some love. As I'm cooing at them, the front door open and closes and my eyes fly to the hallway. He was here the whole time just listening, probably wanting to come to me, but I wouldn't let him. That breaks my heart even more, pushing me farther down into my despair.

Later that day, I move to the front porch to sit with the dogs. Neither has left my side. I mindlessly noting time is standing still for me. My phone has gone off a few times with Nick's name flashing across the screen, but I don't answer. I don't want to talk to anyone. I did call Jaycee like I promised and she's texted me throughout the day. My conflicted emotions get the best of me as I stare across Nick's land. No matter how hard I try, I can't seem to completely close my heart off to him. With a heavy sigh, I go back inside with the intention of fixing myself a hot cup of tea.

When Nick's truck pulls up in front of the cabin, I hold my breath. His footsteps sound along the porch, and I wait for the door to open, praying it doesn't but at the same time, praying it does. His steps stop just outside and then there's nothing but silence. I move towards the door but halt when I hear him retreat. My heart was calling out to him to come in but his didn't hear it.

For the second night in a row, I fall asleep in front of the tree wishing Nick was here with me. My memories go back to looking forward to our future and of starting new traditions. The lights give me a soft sense of peace, but not enough to keep the dreams of heartbreak from causing tears to spill from my eyes as I fight a restless sleep. I want Nick. I need him. Shouldn't I be stronger? Shouldn't I stay away longer? He cheated on me. As I fight my dreams, I wonder what the rule is. How long am supposed to stay away from him? How long until I can forgive him? I want Nick, so I beg the universe to tell me what the damn rule is. Its then I hear my own voice remind me that I'm Abigail McGinty, and I don't like rules.

CHAPTER FIFTEEN

Even in slumber I feel Nick's eyes on me along with a rush of cold air skimming across my body. I didn't hear the truck pull up out front or his footsteps on the porch but I know he's here. The door closes and I shut my eyes and feign sleep. Holding my breath in an attempt to mask my whimpers of relief, I stay completely still when he picks me up and carries me into the bedroom and gently lays me down on the bed. I run my cheeks against the soft cool cotton of the sheets, trying to calm the heat radiating off my skin.

Next, the chandelier is dimmed to almost nothing more than a drop of light, but that tiny drop still has the power of spreading across the entire room, leaving a glow. I sense Nick as he makes his way to the bed. His touch on my cheek is soft but as powerful as the drop of light. My head is telling me to jerk away, but my heart; oh my heart wants his touch. My heart wins when I lean into him. Maybe I'm weak, but I want my Nick. I came here for him. I need to fight for him. He was mine. He says he's mine. He. Is. Mine. I need to forgive or at least try.

We need to get it all out at one time and only then will I know if I can truly forgive him and decide whether we move on together or I need to make my way back to San Antonio. Even if he's mine, I may have to let him go.

I move over, giving him room. He only hesitates a moment before lying down beside me. We're both on our sides, facing each other. I can't stop my hand from reaching over and touching his face. His skin is on fire, just like mine. I flatten my palm and run it along his neck, my eyes following its path. God, I just need to touch him. It feels like an eternity since we've been together. I need to make sure he's still here and real, even though I know it's going to make my pain soar into the Heavens.

His breathing is rapid and jerky and I can see the pulse in his neck thumping and mine is doing the same. Nothing but our heartbeats can be heard or felt in the soft light of the room. Finally, I look up into his eyes and like mine; they're glassy with unshed tears. He sucks in his lips trying to control his emotion. I feel his pain because it's stronger than mine. I love him. I know right at this moment I can't live without Nick.

CHAPTER SIXTEEN

"Tell me what happened," I whisper, but Nick doesn't speak. His only response is to shake his head. "Please, tell me," I whisper again. "I just want us to get past this and move on." Finally, he speaks and his voice causes all the energy to leave my body.

"I'm sorry," Nick says, completely broken. "I didn't mean for anything to happen. I hadn't heard your voice, your laugh, and your words for weeks. I couldn't forget you for a second but I thought you forgot me, Abigail," he speaks so softly I'm not sure if I heard his voice or the pain of his memory.

"Nick," I whisper, "I'm so sorry." I slide close to him until our bodies are almost one. When Nick takes in a deep breath, I hold mine. Here's the part that going to hurt. I stay quiet, holding him tight as he breaks my heart.

"I went into town. I've been walking around lost since leaving you in San Antonio." He hesitantly reaches out to pull me closer. When I let him, he goes on. "I wound up at a bar and started throwing shots down trying to drink away your memory, literally. I thought we were over. I remember talking to Delta. Darcy's sister. Darlin', all I did was talk about you. I got sick and passed out like the lovesick fool I am. That's all I really remember. I know in my heart, darlin' that I wouldn't have done anything else. It was all about you."

What Nick is confessing is confusing. I'm not making sense of his words. I try to grasp on to what he's saying as he continues.

"Delta must have called Darcy. She came into town, picked me up and was able to get me back here and cleaned up." His body tenses. He's just turned into steel, anger radiating off him. "The very next morning you fucking called, goddamn it! The very next fucking morning, Abigail!" he whisper yells and sits up on edge of the bed. *Oh my god. He's livid.* "I couldn't answer, not yet. I was hungover and I didn't want you to hear me like that. I went into town to run an errand for my dad and I was feeling better. I was going to call you as soon as I got back home, but I ran into that fucking bitch, Ashley. She started talking shit. She saw Delta and me. She told me she saw us getting cozy and head out to the parking lot. I told her nothing happened between us and to fuck off, but she told me something did. That she saw everything and had pictures. I told her to show me the fucking pictures and she said only if I went out with her. Told me she'd keep her mouth shut for a night alone with me. She tried to fucking blackmail me into having sex with her. Said she'd post them on the internet. Show them all over town. Embarrass Delta and her family. I've tried to talk to Delta, but she isn't answering any of my calls. I can't find her," he confesses. "But fuck, nothing happened. I don't remember any of that. I don't know."

"Wait! What?! Are you serious?! You don't actually know if anything happened between the two of you? I've been going out of my mind these last two days imagining all these horrible scenarios and you might not have done anything at all?" I ask, completely bewildered.

Nick frowns as he gives a slow nod. "Then you called again. I didn't answer because I was ashamed and worried. I had no idea if she was was telling the truth or not. I didn't want you to hate me. I was going to try and live without you, at least knowing you wouldn't hate me, but you called again. All I could think about was how I wanted you here with me and to hell with everything else. Maybe it was okay if you hated me as long as I had just a few more days with you, to touch you, kiss you and love you, so I finally called. But fucking hell, one day. Not even a day, it was fucking hours and none of this would have happened," he groans.

Something is fishy here. I would think one would remember having sex in a parking lot no matter how drunk. Who is this Ashley bitch? I aim to find out. I'm going to talk to Star and Darcy tomorrow. I slide onto his lap, straddle him and wrap my arms around him.

"Nick, stop," I say softly trying not to strain my voice anymore than it is. I hold onto him even though his hands go to release my arms from around him. "No. Don't leave," I plead. "Please," I beg.

"Let go, darlin'. After what Star said at the store, I know those bitches are up to something and I'm losing my fucking mind thinking they're going to turn you against me," Nick says through gritted teeth, his body vibrating with anger. "Need to walk away for a few minutes." His actions betray his words as he releases my arms to draw me into his embrace.

"No. No more walking away. No more time apart trying to figure things out without each other. Not for another second." I bring his face down to mine.

"One fucking day, fire. One fucking day. I'm so sorry." He buries his face in my neck.

"I love you, Nick," I tell him as I lean down and kiss the spot on his chest over his heart. I feel his shaking at my touch, settling his anger so I go back for more. I know I should wait and I'm probably setting myself up for more emotional tragedy but I'm going with my instinct.

"Abigail," he groans as his hands travel up my back and grip my hair, tugging it so far back my head is arched to a point it's almost painful. Before I can complain or even let out a whimper, he lowers his head and his mouth attacks mine. Like a man starved and I'm his meal, he kisses and bites my neck and shoulders. And, like a man dying of thirst and I'm his water, he's drinking from me to save his life. When he gently bites my bottom lip, I gasp. The intensity of his kiss is almost frightening but I need it. It's rough and painful and still I want more. I'm only along for the ride now. He's in complete control and I happily surrender to him.

Yes, to heal my heartbreak, I allow my body to relax and go completely soft. When he feels me give in, he growls. Next thing I know, my back is on the bed and I'm stripped of his shirt and my panties so quickly it's almost like it didn't happen. Nick comes down and attacks my mouth again. I feel him struggling to get his boxers off and I start to help but his motions are so brutal I decide to stay out of his way and let him do what he's doing. I trust him to take us where we need to be. Before I can catch a breath between his kisses, his fingers find me and start exploring making me wet; then they're in me. I lose my breath again, my hips fly up to meet his fingers as one then two began moving in and out of me. When he feels I'm wet and ready, without warning he's over me and in me in one long hard thrust. We both groan at the feeling of our connection and then still. My breasts are pressed against his chest so I rub my hands up his sides as his lips gently trail kisses along my cheeks and chin. We stay just like that, with only our breathing causing movement. We stay connected, holding each other tight for what seems like hours.

"This, darlin', with you, inside you, is my home. The only place I ever want to be," he says before slowly starting to move his hips. At first his movements are slow, like we're brand new and we've never been together. Like it's our first time. It's intense. It doesn't take long for his thrusts to become stronger, faster and frantic. I can feel he's close and I'm ready too but all of a sudden he pulls out of me. He lowers himself down my body, kissing and gently biting me as he goes down and then his mouth is on me. "Not yet. I need you all night, darlin'," he says while driving me crazy with his mouth and fingers. For the rest of the night we rediscover each other. Taking each other to the edge but refusing to go over and end our connection. Nick runs his hands and mouth over every inch of my body. Not one spot, from my little toe to my eye lids goes untouched. Next, it's my turn. I treat his body to the same attention. Not one spot is missed as I touch and kiss his beautiful body and take him in my mouth, loving his taste. His moans tell me he likes what I'm doing and when I feel him swell, I take him deeper. He tugs my hair and I release him and make my way back up his body. I find his mouth and he pulls my legs up so I straddle him. Releasing his mouth, I rise to a sitting position, lifting up enough to place him at my entrance and with my eyes never leaving his; I slowly lower myself onto him. When he's filled me to the hilt, I stay still, loving the feeling of being full of him. His fingers dig into my hips, and I begin rocking back and forth. Watching him as he's watching me is beautiful and intimate. I moan when his hands grip my hips tighter taking over and controlling my movements. My breath hitches and I cry out when he jerks his hips up, slamming deep into me over and over again.

Right when it becomes too much, his movements slow and he slides his hands up my sides and around to my breast. He runs his fingers over my hardened nipples, gently pinching them, causing me to grind down on him harder. He sits up and kisses me before lowering his mouth to tease and torture my nipples with his tongue and teeth. We're at a point we can't come back from but we're still trying to hold on. Teetering on the edge, our movements slow to a stop and our breathing becomes strained. We roll so he's on top, only our lips and hands are moving. I give him one last hard kiss, holding his head to me, telling him we'll be okay. When we pull back, I look up at him and he's watching me. Our eyes stay connected as we begin moving and only seconds later we fall off the edge together. I call out his name as he whispers mine. The intimacy, not our climax is what we both needed tonight and we found it. My body goes soft but I refuse to let go of him. Neither of us releases our hold on one another. After our breathing settles, Nick slides off to my side, never letting go. I glance at the windows and see dawn peeking in. We're both physically and emotionally exhausted, our eyes barely open, but Nick still leans in for another kiss.

"I love you, fire," he says in his last breath before sleep.

"I love you too, honeysuckle," I whisper back knowing without a doubt Nick Callaghan does love me. I allow his warmth and words to wrap me up in a cocoon like the soft and beautiful branches of honeysuckle, before I fall asleep.

CHAPTER SEVENTEEN

My face is resting against warm skin and I can both hear and feel the sound Nick's heartbeat against my cheek. I slide my hand up his chest near his heart where my face is resting. I begin to open my eyes but stop and wince in pain because the skin around my eyes and face feels tight, dry and swollen. It takes a moment but then it all comes back to me. The day light shining through the windows announcing reality causing small tremors to flood throughout my body. Today I have to talk with Darcy and Star. Nick tenses and draws me closer. A few unwelcome tears make their way from my eyes to Nick's chest as I scoot up as far as I can on top of Nick and bury my face in his neck. He holds me tight as both our fears flood back in. Neither of us speak and I'm not sure how long silent tears fall from my eyes because later I wake again only to find Nick's body draped over mine and he's sound asleep. I have to use the bathroom but don't want to move from his warmth but I have no choice. I slide from his arms and he lets out a deep whimper.

"I'll be right back. I need to use the restroom," I tell him softly. Nick sits up in the bed and pulls the covers from us and helps me sit up. As I start to leave the bed, so does Nick. "Where you going? Just stay here and rest. I'll be right back." I tell him and caress his bearded cheek. He ignores me and stands from the bed anyway. Both of us naked, we make our way to the bathroom.

Once inside, Nick leads me to the private area where the toilet is and turns towards the shower. As I go in and close the door, I hear the shower turn on and when I come back out, Nick is just finishing up from brushing his teeth. He tugs me into the warm shower and then hands me his toothbrush full of toothpaste.

"Are you trying to tell me something?" I try to smile and joke, but the humor is absent from my voice. When he hears my voice is still scratchy, he touches my throat. His gaze holds mine before his eyes travel down, following the path of his fingers as they caress the skin along my throat. He looks back into my eyes and frowns, still not speaking. He shakes his head and pulls me into the water's mist. After I brush my teeth, Nick grabs the soap and begins washing my body. Like his kisses last night, not one part of my body goes untouched. Next he washes my hair, taking extra time to rub my head and neck. I relax into him while

126

he does it. After rinsing me off, I stop him from exiting the shower. I do what I did last night, what he just did for me. I wash his body and hair while giving him tiny kisses of reassurance that will let him know we're going to be okay. We dry off and head back to the bed and lay down. Both of us are exhausted but we need to eat.

"What time is it?" I ask softly, snuggling back into him. He reaches for his phone on the nightstand, and picks it up to where we can both look at the screen. It's almost eight in the morning, time for breakfast. "Let's get dressed, baby. Let's go have breakfast with your parents. Do you think Darcy and Star will be there?"

His eyes full of worry come to mine. I know he's scared. Scared of letting me go and me finding out what he doesn't remember and something happened. I don't want to be stuck in this heartbreak though. I can't believe I'm the strong one here but I'm the one who's going to have to convince him we have to face this head on Maybe this is God's way of healing me. Distracting me from my own pain and showing me how strong my love is for my honeysuckle just like Jaycee and Blue so I try again. "My sweet honeysuckle. We're going to be okay," I say and lean over and kiss his cheek. "Just give us time to figure it out and let's find our closure," I kiss his neck. "I love you, Nick." I rise up and look at him. "Tell me you love me, please," I beg softly as I lean down and kiss his lips. His hand reaches up and grasps the back of my head pulling me in hard for a kiss. His tongue desperate to taste me and mine just as needy. I pull back just enough to whisper against his lips. "Tell me," I plead. In an instant he's on top of me, kissing me. He pulls back, not wanting to hurt me. When he stops to look in my eyes I say again, "Please, tell—" is all I get out before he's kissing me again.

"I am telling you," he finally whispers and continues his affections. When he finally speaks, I let out a sigh of relief and run my fingers through his hair, tugging him closer. We're making out like teenagers but soon we're broken apart by a banging on the door. We both look at the hallway and then Nick drops his head down on mine. "Abigail?" he whispers. We sit up but he keeps me straddling him, his arms tight around my back and his face buried against my neck. I hold him close for a couple of seconds before lacing my fingers in his hair and tugging his head back so he looks at me.

"We're going to be fine. Let's go start our life, Nick," I reassure him, looking directly into his eyes. The more he loves me the more I know that Ashley is a liar.

He searches my face for only a second before getting out of bed. "I'll be right back," he tells me as he tugs on a pair of sweatpants. I give him a real smile and nod, showing him it's okay.

After he leaves, I sit up on the edge of the bed and listen as Nick makes it to the front door and opens it. It only takes me a moment before I recognize Huck, Levi, Darcy and Star's voices. I get up and quickly go over to my suitcases. I rummage through both of them for something to wear. I grab a pair of panties and a bra, knee high winter socks, an old pair of Levi's and a white long sleeved thermal shirt to wear under my super soft and thick blue and white checkered flannel shirt. I'm dressed with my boots on and in the bathroom brushing my hair when Nick comes back into the room. He joins me and stands behind me, wrapping his arms tight around my waist. I meet his gaze in the reflection of the mirror and smile. When he doesn't return it, I set the brush down and turn around in his arms and hold him close.

"Let's go eat, honeysuckle." My voice is still strained and I grimace. Hearing me obviously upsets him and until it heals, he's going to be in a bad way. He gives me a reluctant nod and walks back out into the bedroom. When I finish brushing my hair I put it in a loose braid that wraps around my neck. Nick is sitting on the edge of the bed dressed and pulling on his boots. All that crosses my mind is how handsome he is, nothing else. He's that beautiful.

He looks up at me as he rests his elbows on his knees, "Are we really okay?" he mumbles, unsure. "We're going to be," I answer and comb his still damp hair with my fingers. He relaxes a little and closes his eyes. When I'm done, he looks up at me before wrapping his arms around my waist and resting his head against my stomach. Yes, my big strong Nick needs me this time. I'll save him the way he saved me.

CHAPTER EIGHTEEN

We exit the cabin and make our way down the steps to the truck. While walking, I ask Nick where everyone went. He takes my hand and pulls me to his side of the truck while explaining their meeting us up at his parent's place. He opens the door so I hop in and scoot over just enough so I'm sitting in the middle next to Nick and after a couple of attempts the old truck's cold engine starts and soon we're pulling up to the back of his parent's beautiful home. The back of the house is much like the front with columns holding up the second story balcony. The first floor patio has five arches that open to a stone patio. Some parts of the outside look like Spanish colonial while others look a traditional southern plantation. As we head up the stone path, I notice four chimneys rising from the roof with smoke billowing from them and the air smells amazing. I've always loved the smell of wood burning so I give myself a moment to take it in. We reach the covered porch and I marvel at the beautiful double glass doors with a wrought iron design embedded in their glass. Before we head inside, I catch Nick's eyes and see he's still worried.

"Are you sure?" he asks again.

I'm embarrassed his parents saw us the way they did last night but I shake it off and give him my best smile and nod. We step into a mudroom where everyone's coats are hung. Nick and I take ours off and hang them only to turn around and see everyone has stopped what they were doing and are staring at us. I tuck myself into Nick's side and wait for someone to say something. I glance over and see Darcy and Star and I know I need to reach out to them. My thoughts sidetracked when Levi gets up and moves around the kitchen.

"So, Abigail, how do you like your coffee?" he asks and grabs for a mug from the counter. Before looking at me for an answer, he looks at Nick and then winks at me.

"I'll get it for her," Nick says and finally shakes a little bit of last couple of days off as he pulls us towards the coffee pot, bumping Levi in the shoulder in the process. I don't turn around but I can hear chuckles and giggles. I reach my arm around Nick's waist and pull him to me as he drapes his arm around my shoulder. At the sound of clanking, I twist my upper body in time to take some silverware Nick's dad, Ronan, is handing us.

"Kept the food warm. Go get you some," he says and points to a buffet counter.

Nick and I were so caught up in one another that when I finally turn and see everyone watching us, I become embarrassed. It only takes a second for me to shake it off when I see Lincoln and Lina Jennings standing with everyone in the kitchen. "Oh, my God! Ms. Jennings?" I whisper "Abigail, it's so good to see you," Ms. Jennings sweet voice rings out. I look into her eyes. They're so different now. She's always been beautiful but now there's a light about her. Her eyes, they're bright and almost dancing.

"Hey, Abigail. It's so good to see you," Linc mumbles and I smile. "Hey, Linc."

After all that went down with his brother Rocky and my sister, Jaycee, one would think there would be animosity between the families but there's not. I look at Ms. Jennings again with questions in my eyes "We'll talk more later. For now, I'll just say that there's an amazing group of young doctors at Texas Tech that I owe a lot to.

Right now, you both need to eat." Lina finishes and points to the buffet.

China, Nick's mom steps up. "Come on, you two, need y'all to eat before my heart can settle." she halfway jokes. Nick comes up behind me and leads me to the buffet that's sitting along the back kitchen wall. While he's making a plate, I take in my surroundings. This kitchen is so cool. Very country. I glance over and see Nick watching me and I feel shy. He notices because he stands closer to me while smiling and hands me the plate before reaching for another. I look down and start to panic. A huge pile of scrambled eggs are topped with four pieces of bacon and hash browns are piled on it. And, for good measure, he's added two biscuits.

"Woooh, cowboy. How about we make this your plate?" I ask and switch plates with him and head over to a bowl of fresh fruit.

Nick sets his plate down on the island and comes back to the buffet and takes my plate from me. I almost say something but when he heads for the bowl of fruit, I relax. After Nick puts a spoonful of fruit on it, I reach for it, but he's not done. A frown forms on my lips as he loads my plate with cantaloupe, melon, strawberries and grapes but after he goes in for a fourth spoonful I gently touch his arm to stop him. He looks over at me and I tilt my head.

"That's good. Thank you," I whisper in warning and reach for my plate before he can add a side of beef to it. After dropping half of the fourth spoonful on top he smirks. I narrow my eyes on him and his smirk turns into a smug grin when he finally hands it to me. I almost say something but I decide to pick my battles and do my best to eat this gigantic pile of fruit on my plate. It's doable and I'm just glad to see his cocky smirk and teasing side come back out a little.

Chatter fills the room as I sit down on a barstool at the counter. I fork up some melon and plop it in my mouth as I look around. Nick and I are the only ones eating. Everyone else must have already had their breakfast because they're standing around and only half of them have coffee mugs in their hands and are talking about the weather. Nick settles next to me on the barstool and I place my hand on his thigh as I keep shoveling fruit in my mouth. I sense someone beside me and look over my shoulder to see Ronan setting two bowls next to my plate. One has yogurt and the other has granola. I'm about protest when Nick chuckles. He just shrugs, and I again start to protest, stopping when Ronan jabs a finger at my fruit.

"That's ridiculous. You're too skinny. If you're going to insist on only eating fruit, you'll eat the other too. It's high in calories and will put some fat on you." Ronan insists inviting no argument.

But poor Ronan, he doesn't know me. I sigh as I drop my fork to my plate and turn to face him on my stool. Everyone has gone quiet.

"With all due respect, Mr. Callaghan, those are the very reasons I do not eat yogurt or granola. I will also add that I've been making my own plates and picking my own food since I could walk and talk," I say, my voice still a little hoarse. I glance back at Nick who has been watching us while chuckling but he quickly turns back at his own plate.

"Listen here, young lady, a healthy breakfast is important. And call me Ronan," he snaps at me and then turns his back to me. I can't see what he's doing, but I don't have long to wonder when plops a plate of bacon down beside me before continuing his lecture. "And you forgot a food group."

My jaw drops. "I did not 'forget' a food group, *Ronan*. I do not want any bacon," I reply and jab my finger at the plate.

"You don't like bacon? How can you not like bacon?" Ronan asks, almost offended.

"I didn't say I didn't like bacon. I said I didn't want any bacon," I toss back at him in a hiss.

"You're one of those vegan types, aren't you?" he asks while narrowing his eyes on me.

Now I'm offended. "Oh, good Lord." I reach down and grab a piece of bacon off the plate and take a huge bite. "No!" I bark softly around the bacon. "Happy now?" I ask while angrily chomping down the rest of my bacon. I watch as a huge smile, almost identical to Nick's, spreads across his face and I can't help but smile back. I didn't realize how much I was missing my dad, Stone, until being around Ronan. It's going to be nice to have someone to drive crazy.

"Yes, darlin'. Now, I'm happy," he says and walks over to the counter and picks his mug of coffee up and takes a sip.

Nick's still shoveling food into his mouth with a huge smile on his face and his body is shaking with laughter as he chews his food. I stab another piece of fruit with my fork and as I chew, I notice everyone is laughing. I glare at Nick's dad, and then smile my sweetest smile at his mom. "Thank you so much for breakfast, Mrs. Callaghan," I say to only her and everyone starts laughing.

"Oh, she's going to fit in just fine with this family," Star says to Darcy and Darcy agrees with a nod through her silent laughter.

"You're welcome, sweet pea, and please, call me China," Mrs. Callaghan, China, replies before coming over with two mugs of coffee and placing them on the counter in front of Nick and I. A man I didn't even notice was in the room walks up and places a carton of creamer and a bowl of sugar in front of us. *How in the hell did I not notice him?*

"Here you go, sweetheart." He's certainly one of the hottest older men I've ever seen. I feel like I've just been slapped by a dumb stick because I can't speak. He's covered in tattoos at least what I can see that's not covered by clothing. He's wearing a black Henley that's pushed up to his elbows and faded blue jeans with motorcycle boots. He's got to be close to my dad's age, but for some reason the fact that I find this man outrageously hot is not grossing me out.

"Thank you," I finally stammer out. He nods and grins at me before taking Lina's mug from her, refilling it and then handing it back to her.

"Here you go, babe," he says and a blush covers her cheeks. Lincoln rolls his eyes but grins behind his mug as he takes another sip of his coffee.

"Thank you, Red." she says bashfully.

Oooooooh, so this is Red. Interesting.

"Okay, everyone let them eat." At China's request, everyone starts talking.

Nick's hand comes down on my knee and squeezes. He's smiling at me, but it's a weary smile. "I love you, honeysuckle," I say to try and erase his anxiety. He squeezes my knee again and then keeps his hand there as we finish our breakfast.

Once we're done eating and all plates are rinsed and placed in the dishwasher, China looks over at Darcy, Star and I who have been sitting quietly watching our men chat. "Girls, y'all go on and show Abigail around the house. All the ends and outs and secret passageways around this old place." She smiles. "Those two, along with Huck and Nick, have been playing hide-and-seek in this house since they could walk. Levi came a little while later and they still played around this place even as teenagers. Lost them a couple of times," she laughs. "Lina and I are going to chat and enjoy another cup of coffee while we can. Now that the snow has stopped, the sky cleared and the sun is up and bright. It's going to be melting off the snow but not fast enough. Tonight's freezing temps are going to turn that melting snow into ice and that's dangerous. None of us need to be out in that so the men need to check on the livestock and property and they might be a while. Don't want y'all out it that so find something to do until they get back," she tells us as she settles in a chair next to Lina.

"I can stay." Nick offers after making his way over to me.

"No, go on. I want to see the house and you need to help everyone. I'll be fine and I'll be waiting," I lean up and kiss him. He kisses me back but stops abruptly before grabbing my hand and dragging me out of the kitchen, through a living area where a big beautiful Christmas tree is lit up, and keeps going. We pass under an archway that leads into a huge foyer. I only get a quick glance around, noticing two glossy wooden benches sitting on either side of a huge wood double door and a wide staircase with a wood banister with spiral spindals leading up to a second floor, before my back is pushed up against a wall and Nick's lips are on mine. After a passionate kiss, he pulls back. "I don't want to leave you," he whispers.

"Nick, it's going to be okay," I assure him. "I'll be right here, waiting," I follow with what I know are the most powerful promise and one I never have intention of breaking. "I promise. I'll be right here, honeysuckle," I tell him with all the love and serenity I can muster. Nick searches my face for a few seconds before nodding. He believes me and gives me another quick kiss before we return to the kitchen.

"We'll be a while but hopefully back by dinner. Got to run over to Linc's too," Nick informs me. "Signals are bad when we're in the field but you should be okay." He approaches his dad, Red, Levi, Huck and Linc who already have their coats on and are waiting. Nick looks back at me and I give him one final smile before he grabs his coat from the hook in the mudroom and follows the others out. When he opens the door to leave, Buford and Elvis make their way in. They sit down on their haunches by the back door and wait. I grin as I walk over to them while looking around for something to wipe off their paws. The same style hamper Nick has is by the door so I open it and grab a towel from inside before I kneel down in front of them. Both dogs lead me through the process of cleaning their paws and then snuggle up against me. I give them each a head rub before glance out the back door just in time to see

Nick standing by the door of a huge truck with Huck behind the wheel. He gives me a slight wave that I return and then he hops in the truck and I watch as they drive off.

CHAPTER NINETEEN

I walk back into the kitchen and Darcy and Star make their way to me. "Let's go have a look-see. What do you say?" Star asks and takes my hand, pulling me behind her as we head towards the foyer.

I stop both of them. I have to do it. My stomach flips when I glimpse at them before looking away. "I need to talk to you both. I need your help. It's about Nick." I chance another peek. Their loyalty is for Nick, their lifelong friend. And of course we're talking about Darcy's sister. Asking them is risky but I'm sensing I'll get an honest answer and an alley against Ashley.

"Of course." Star agrees and nods and pulls me behind her again. "Let's go upstairs. We can sit around and gossip." She and Darcy both giggle.

Great! Nick and I can be their topic today.

As we pass through the larger than life living area I stop and look around. It's huge. Despite its size, the room has a warm feel. This tree is taller than the one at the cabin and is decorated with red and white lights and different shaped gold ornaments. Some are plain round bulbs; some are shaped as crosses, and some angels. Large red and gold beads wind around the tree from top to bottom and a brilliant gold star sits at the top. The skirt is a beautiful gold with red trim and an electric train tracks circle the skirt. The train is lit up in bright colors with Santa sitting front and center on the engine. A gingerbread man is riding on the caboose and tons of candy and elves cover the middle cars. I turn to the fireplace where a fire is glowing and take in the mantel. It's lined with framed photos and garland with a giant reef hanging above it. The tables are all decorated with red and gold candles and poinsettia plants, more than a dozen are spaced out around the room.

"I love poinsettias," I utter and keep looking around.

"China and Ronan's mothers, they were both born in December and they both loved poinsettia plants. Every Christmas she buys as many as she can and spreads them throughout the house in their memory and in celebration of their birthdays," Darcy shares.

"That's a beautiful sentiment," I reply and smile as I make a mental note to make sure and fill my tin tubs with them for Nick.

"So what's all this talk about hiding spots and stuff?" I get side tracked from my problems with Nick when my thoughts return to the mysterious comments about the house.

"Not exactly sure why Nick's granddaddy added secret passages, but it's rumored it had something to do with prohibition. Others say it was because of the train robbers who hit the area in the early 1900's. The robbers would kill the passengers and just toss their bodies out over the trestle like they were trash." Star explains. "If their spoils weren't enough, they'd sometimes drift further out into the country. They came looking for more loot on the ranches," she whispers dramatically and then laughs before she goes on. "They began robbing homes and murdering the residents. Those murders had the town terrified. Devil worshipping was even rumored to be going on and rituals were happening. People were disappearing and being found murdered in crazy ways with markings on their corpses like they were being sacrificed." She glances around before continuing. "They say Nick's granddaddy built this house so if intruders entered, the family could

145

hide and also arm themselves with weapons that was placed at different spots inside the house and behind the walls. At least that what the rumors say."

I hadn't even realized I had stopped moving and was staring at Star with my jaw hanging down and fear across my face. I glance at Darcy and she's smiling.

"Is she joking?" I pray she is.

Darcy laughs and shrugs her shoulders. "That just what's rumored. I don't know," she answers with a grin pulling at the corners of her mouth.

"Y'all are so, so wrong," I say through a nervous laugh and they burst out laughing.

We all jump and scream when Buford and Elvis begin barking loudly. Darcy grabs her chest.

"Shit," Star says and sits down on the steps. "I was telling the story and that still scared me half to death."

"What in the world is wrong with you girls?" China calls out.

"Nothing. We're okay," Star calls back on a breathless laugh.

The dogs are whimpering and scratching on the back door so I walk over to them, still shaken by the story. "They must have to go out again," I mutter standing in the mudroom where both dogs are looking out the back door at something. Not seeing anything, I give them both a quick head rub which usually gets me some love but they're too focused on going outside. With a shaky hand, I open the door and they take off faster than I've ever seen either of them move while barking like crazy. "Okay, that's scary. Maybe there's a squirrel or raccoon out there and not train robbers or devil worshippers coming to take me and use as a sacrifice," I say to myself as I close the door and make my way back to the staircase when Darcy and Star are waiting.

"How about some good stories?" Darcy asks.

"Yeah, that would be much better. Thanks," I reply and start back up the stairs.

"We had so many good times here." Darcy begins. Star turns around and looks back at Darcy.

"It was my haven after I lost my parents." she agrees and sadness takes over her expression. I can't help but wonder what happened to her parents. "You lost your parents?" I blurt out like an idiot. "I'm sorry, Star."

"No, its okay a tornado hit the area a while back. My momma and daddy, they were traveling in their truck back from working in town and had nowhere to go." She shakes her head as though trying to clear her mind as anguish flashes across her face but soon it's replaced with a sweet sentiment as she goes on. "But they're still with me. My momma taught me how to make a mean peach cobbler and my daddy taught me to aim like no one's business "I'm the sharpest shooter in this county and three surrounding counties and I'm always packing. Never go anywhere without my gun and sleep with one under my pillow." She pulls up the hem of her sweater and points to her belt buckle. It's the same one I saw her wearing at Wal-Mart. The huge one with a skull and two revolvers coming off the sides. "This was first prize trophy at last year's local competition. My daddy would be proud. I miss them and I'm so thankful for each moment I had with them.

"I'm so sorry, Star. I'm so sorry for your loss. I hope I didn't upset you too much."

"No, I'm okay. Thank you. Their deaths were hard on me. Talking about them, it's a beautiful thing. Not talking about them in hope to avoid the pain, it doesn't work."

We walk up the rest of the stairs and when we reach the landing there's a beautiful antique style side table lining the walls with picture frames on top. I step closer and take in some of the pictures. Some are black and whites and date back quite a while judging by the way the people are dressed in the photos. One is of Nick and Star and a little giggle escapes when I take in his crazy curly hair and freckled face. They're both in swimsuits and Nick has his arm draped around her shoulder.

"I was going to marry him." She smiles and laughs. "Boy, did I chase him, and boy did he run from me and he could run fast." Darcy laughs and collectively we all start to move to the couches in their loft.

"So he ran too fast for you?" I laugh again.

"I ran faster and one day caught him. We were about eleven years old and I'd convinced him he would marry me come hell or high water and to just give up the fight. He looked so defeated. I told him that we were officially engaged to be married and he had to kiss me. Poor Nick looked like I was leading him to the guillotine but he finally gave in and kissed me. Gross." She shudders.

"I convinced both of us that kissing was just disgusting in general and that we'd still get married, but it turned out my heart and kisses were fickle. When Huck came back from summer vacation our eighth grade year, oh boy, puberty, he had reached it or better yet, puberty had hit him like a Mac truck after a football game, he pulled me behind the scoreboard and kissed me. With him I did see fireworks and hear angels sing. Huck, he's the only one for me."

I look over at Darcy almost in question. I'm interested in learning both their history with Nick. I can tell we're all going to be good friends but I need to ask her about her sister and that night. "And you and Nick? Y'all are very close." I ask her and a sweet smile comes across her lips. We sit on the couch, with Star and me taking the biggest and Darcy settling on the smallest. She tugs off her boots and tosses them to the side and then tucks her feet up and underneath herself as she settles; with Star following suit. They really do feel at home here. I sit there feeling a little awkward when Star reaches over and grabs my leg tossing it across her lap and pulling off my boot. I start laughing before reaching down to yank off my other boot at the same time she reaches for it. "Okay, okay, I got it. Thanks," I say and toss my other boot next to hers and Darcy's.

"Wait." Star stands and walks over to the wall and pushes against a panel. There's a click and then it pops open. She reaches in and opens an inner door and comes back with three bottles of cherry Coke and settles back on the couch and passes out the bottles.

I look back over at the panel and tilt my head looking for any marks that would let someone know that's there.

"It's cool, huh?" Star asks me and I nod in disbelief. I never would have noticed that if she wouldn't have done that. "There are things like that all over the place. Hidden rooms, passages and wall panels that just pop open. We'll have to show you everything, but first what did you want to talk to us about?"

"Okay." My heart and stomach do a flip as I begin. "Remember how you warned me about Ashley?" Star and Darcy make a sound that reminds me of a lioness ready to attack. Okay? Just do it. Ask.

"She told Nick she had pictures of Delta and him having sex in a parking lot." I blurt out and wait for my heart to be ripped into shreds.

Star and Darcy both do a head jerk and then burst out laughing.

"What?" Star wipes her eyes but then a look of calm fury that scares me takes over her expression.

"Before I came here, I had pushed Nick away for a time." My eyes fall in regret.
"We know." Darcy reaches over and lays a comforting hand on my leg. "But you're here now."

"Nick told me he went into town one night. Got really drunk. The night you had to get him?" Darcy nods.

"I remember. Delta called. She would have brought him home, but she had to be somewhere."

"So what does this have to do with Ashley?" Star growls.

"She approached Nick and told him that she had pictures of him and Delta having sex in the parking lot. He was too drunk to remember. I mean he says he didn't but now he's doubtful because he was pretty messed up."

"Are you serious?" Darcy pulls out her phone. "I'm calling her."

"There's no way." Star chimes in.

"She's not answering and hasn't for a few days. My dad and she are up to something. I'm worried about her. But I will find out." Darcy promises, pocketing her phone.

"I'd be worried too." Star confides.

"Why?" I press.

"My parents are not good people. I live with my grandpa in a home at the back of our property because I can barely tolerate being around them. They want me back in the main house and think I'm wasting my life away as a nurse. My dad has these crazy ideas about taking over West Texas and part of that goal is for me to marry Nick Callaghan, the Cattle Prince. He wants to combine the cotton and ranching industry in these parts to create a monopoly. He's insane and won't let go of that idea. I'm in love with Levi and have been since high school. My dad has been keeping us apart for years. But now, Levi's finally staying. Says we're going to get married. I can't wait," she says excitedly.

"We'll get it all cleared up, Abigail. Nick wouldn't have done that. He loves you. All he talked to any of us about was you. Nick never ever bound himself to anyone until you came along. Not because he's some type of player but because he's a good man. He would never lead anyone on. Girls in this town like that about him. No bull and no promises. Of course there are a couple of women like Ashley that almost stalked him hoping to get his ring on their finger, but he's never given those types of girls a second look." Star reassures me.

I stare at them before standing and walking over and grabbing my boots.

"Hey, what are you doing?" Star asks.

"I'm going to find Ashley and kicking her ass." I promise and rush for the stairs.

"Wait for us!" Star calls out.

Halfway down the stairs, the house shakes with a loud boom. It startles me, rattling my thoughts and I fall down in shock. Dazed, I start back up the stairs, feeling disoriented. *What the hell was that?* Then I hear yelling. I expect to hear Lina or China calling out for us but it's not. It's a man. A man with a Spanish accent and he's threatening to kill everyone if they move. I try to stand but fall again so I start dragging my body up the stairs when I see Darcy and Star at the top of the stairs on their belly's reaching out for me. Once I get close enough I reach out to them and they grab my hands and begin pulling me up the rest of way. They keep pulling me until we're halfway down the hallway while the man continues shouting.

"Who else is in the house?" he demands.

China speaks up, her voice terrified. "No one. Just us. It's just us. What do you want?" she screams in anger but fear is laced in her voice.

"I want Abigail McGinty and Lincoln Jennings," he answers, his voice seething with hatred.

"What? Why?" Lina asks.

The man laughs. "Why? Because the Sombra, he's an angel oscuro and he's killing off my family. He killed my brother, many of my men and my SON!!" he bellows. "I am here to stop him. I'm here to destroy what's trying to destroy me. This Ángel oscuro defies death or lives after, I don't know but I will have my revenge," he says with malice.

"Who are you talking about?" Lina asks through a shaky voice.

"You know who I'm talking about. He is your hijo. He is like a demon cat. He has many lives, like a cat, but he is finally going to run out," his voice now laced with humor.

"My son, Lincoln?" Lina asks, confused. "He's done nothing. We live here. Bother no one. Leave us alone," she pleads.

"No, not Lincoln, but he will die for his brother's sins. No, Madre, I'm speaking of your hijo, Rocky. This time he dies for good."

CHAPTER TWENTY

Rocky? I don't have time to gather my thoughts when the man goes on with his threats.

"I will kill him a hundred times within a minute to assure myself he will never be back," he spits his words out.

I join hand with Darcy and Star and we retreat down the hall. "Rocky's dead," Lina says sadly.

"No, Madre, he is not and if I'm guessing right, he'll come soon if he's not already here," the man replies, followed by the scraping of a chair. "So, let just sit and wait."

"Why Abigail?" China asks.

"Oh, Abigail will pay for her sister. Because of Jaycee McGinty, my brother died in that house. Rocky killed him for her. She will pay for her sister's sins. I will be killing two birds with one stone, no? It will only tide me over until I get back to San Antonio. Soon, all the McGinty's and

Bradshaw's will pay. But for now, the Jennings' and Callaghan's are my priority," he informs them. "Let's relax and visit like old friends for a few moments, shall we? I'm sure now that everyone has heard the explosion, they'll all come running. We'll be able to pick them off like fish in a barrel, no?" He laughs and I hear a few more chuckles. He's not alone.

Star is turning the knob on a bedroom door, when we all freeze. "Search the house now. Make sure they're telling the truth. Make sure we're alone," the man orders.

Star leads the way as we enter the last room on the right. I look around in a panic, wondering where we can hide. Voices and footsteps echo up the stairs as Darcy rushes to the closet. The closet? We can't hide in the closet; they'll find us for sure.

The door we passed through opens followed by the sound of the closet doors being open and closed. Like I thought. They're searching the closets. Darcy grabs my hand and drags me into the closet. Star is hiding by some coats that she's pushed aside. She waves us towards her and as I get closer I see it, a hidden panel. She carefully slides it open and waves us in. Darcy goes first and I follow. Once in, Star reaches back and pulls the coats back across the rack and carefully slides the panel closed. Our breathing gets heavier when we hear the men enter the room. The closet door opens and I brace myself, terror gripping me. Star silently bends over, pulling her pant leg up and pulls out a 9MM. I stare at her in awe, wondering how she can be so calm. As quiet as a mouse, she releases the safety. She takes a step back and raises her arms aiming the gun at the sliding panel. If it opens, whoever is on the other side is surely dead. Darcy grabs my hand and we hold on tight as clothes are moved around and boxes pulled from the shelves and dropped. Not once does Star blink or break her stance. Finally, a voice calls out, "Clear," and the footsteps retreat. It takes a few more moments before we all silently let out a breath of relief. Before I can take my next breath, Darcy is pulling me through a narrow passageway and down a flight of stairs. We make our way between the exterior frame and inner walls. The stairs are the only thing that would seem out of place, well that and the space between the frame and inner walls being wide. I know the walls are thin and the only thing between us and them is plywood, so my movements along with Darcy and Star's are quiet as we make our way to down along the walls to the first floor. We come to a halt when we hear voices.

"I want them here now. Blow something else up. If they think they have time, they'll plot, but in their haste we'll be able to kill them easily," the man says.

"The other car, Jefe?" another man ask.

"Si," the one who I now know is the leader says.

"That can also act as a distraction for us," I whisper and they both nod. "One of us needs to try to leave and call the men and tell them they're walking into an ambush."

Our phones. *Shit.* I quickly pull mine out of my pocket and put it on mute in case it rings. Star and Darcy do the same. We go further into the passageway and sit down in a crawl space. Star pulls out her phone again.

"We have a couple of minutes. Keep them on silent but get to texting everyone now," Star whispers.

I text Nick and tell him we need help and people are in the house. My hands are shaking as I stare at the phone waiting but nothing happens. No replies. Darcy shakes her head saying nothing too. Star starts pushing buttons on her phone and then puts it to her ear. Her eyes dart between Darcy and I as she speaks in a whisper. "Callaghan Ranch. This is Starley Henderson. People are in the house. They have guns. They're holding Lina Jennings and China

Callaghan hostage. Help us. We're hiding in the walls," she whispers. The 911 operator must ask who because she says, "Darcy Ramsey, me and Abigail McGinty."

None of us say a thing when we hear a thump overhead. Star hangs up the phone and we all wait. I'm sweating and trying to control my breathing but I'm starting to panic being in this tight, hot space. Darcy senses my panic and takes my hand. Long moments pass before we start crawling along the passageway again, not stopping until we get to a bigger space and finally my breathing calms.

"You two go for help. I have the gun and I'm good to take a few of these assholes out," Star whispers.
"You can't. They'll know someone's in the house. We need to take a few of them out and make sure Lina and China will be safe before we go for the men," I counter and both of them look at me. "Guns. Are there more guns?" I ask.

"Yes. There's enough guns stashed around this house to supply a small army," Star replies.

"Then let's go get them."

"The only ones I know about are all in the main house. We'll have to go back out," Darcy says.

We all stop our whispering when we hear the boss start to talk.

"Get Senor Ramsey. He can make a call to the men. They'll never suspect he's leading them to their deaths. He wants that boy that's been sniffing around his daughter dead."

Darcy's knees buckle. I grab her to hold her up from falling.

"He's requested we make sure he's the first one to go down. Me, eh, I have no preference as long as they all die."

Darcy gasps but quick as lightning Star covers her mouth with her hand stifling the sound. Darcy brings her hands over Star's as her gasp turns into a scream, a scream only we know is happening.

"Senor Ramsey owes me a lot of money and tell him if he does what he's told; I will forgive the debt for half of his failing farm. That should keep his bitch of a wife in her diamonds for a little while longer," he says in disgust and we hear their footsteps fade as they walk away.

Darcy eyes begin to water. I can't imagine what she must be feeling. If a killer is talking about her parents with disgust, they must be far worse than even she imagined. She shakes her head and lowers her hands and Star slowly lowers hers.

"I'll go get the guns. You two stay here," she says and starts back down the hall. Star reaches out for her but Darcy whips around and points at both of us. "No. Y'all are not going out there. I will not allow any harm to come to my friends and Levi because of my parents' greed. If anyone gets hurt or caught, it should be me. They may have mercy on me if I tell them who my father is. Make your way to the attic. I'll meet you there. Keep trying to text the men. Sooner or later they have to head in from the field and their phones are going be lighting up. Y'all need to be able to talk to them," she reminds us before hurrying away.

We watch her go and then Star takes my hand and squeezes it. "Let's go," she whispers with tremendous sadness.

We make our way through the narrow passageways and after about five minutes, Star finally stops and points to a ladder built along the wall. She taps my arm and points up.

"That door leads to the attic," she whispers and begins climbing towards the top.

I hear something and whip around and almost scream but I see it's Darcy and she has definitely found some guns. She has a rifle with its strap hung over her shoulder and she's holding a shotgun in one hand. The other is holding ammo and along the front of her pants she's tucked two handguns. I take the shotgun and rifle from her.

"Head up and I'll hand them off to you and then you can hand them off to Star," I offer and watch as she starts up the ladder. When she reaches the top, she pushes the ammo along the floor of the attic and then does the same with the handguns from her waist before climbing back down. Once she's halfway, she turns back to me. I hold the rifle up to her and she holds it up when Star appears through the hole to grab it. After we repeat the process with the shotgun, Darcy climbs up into the attic and I'm right behind her. I slide on my belly to clear the trap door and then roll over on my back while Darcy closes and locks the latch.

"Hey, I got a message," Star says, and we pull out our phone and start reading our messages. The men are on their way. Thank God. We let out a sigh of relief but then scream as the house shakes from the second explosion. We missed our opportunity and they probably heard our cries.

My phone goes off again while I'm gathering my bearings.

Nick: *What was hell was that? Are y'all okay? Are you okay? We're on our way! Stay hidden*

Me: *They blew up the car out front. Trying to get you to rush here so that they can catch you off guard. We're fine for now but we screamed. They may have heard us. Be careful but please hurry.*

Nick: *I'm coming, baby. I'll be there soon. I love you.*

As I lay there, my breathing heavy I want to just pretend we'll get out of this alive and live happily ever after. Right now I'll just settle for getting out of alive. The rest will come.

CHAPTER TWENTY-ONE

"Which are you most comfortable with?" Star asks. I reach down and grab the .38 special while Darcy grabs the shotgun. Star tucks the .22 in her belt and hooks the strap of the rifle over her shoulder. We peer out the attic window and see Nick's mom's car laying in fiery pieces across the lawn. "Jesus Christ." Star says.

I watch a truck make its way down the long gravel drive leaving a cloud of dust behind it. "Who's that?" I ask. Darcy repositions her shotgun before she answers.

"My father," she responds. The truck slams to a stop and a tall thin man with dark hair, wearing sunglasses and cowboy boots exits the truck. Before he closes the door he reaches in and grabs a black felt Stetson and secures it on his head.

"Senor Ramsey. How nice to see you again." the boss calls out.

"Don't you ever summon me again, Vargas." Darcy's dad snarls.

"Tsk tsk, Vernon. That's not a very nice way of talking to the man who's going to solve all your problems."

"Yeah, when I see it I'll believe it. Right now you're nothing more than another pain in my ass I don't need."

"I'm going." Darcy starts for the trap door.

"No! No way, Darcy," Star grabs her. "We're going to wait for the men to get here."

"No, I'm not. You two are but I'm facing off with my father now." She yanks free of Star's grip.

"Please, Darcy, Don't go down there alone." I plead.

"If he's gone this far to keep me away from Levi, he's desperate. He's willing to do anything and only my safety will get him what he wants. If I go down, I'll also be in a position to make sure no one gets hurt." she tells us and kneels down and undoes the latch on the trap door. As she starts to climb down, Star pulls out a few extra shells of ammunition. She kneels down and hands them to Darcy, who sticks it in her back pocket and begins descending.

When she's out of view, I grab extra ammo for my .38, and Star grabs some extra for her .22. We share a look and then Star starts down the stairs and I follow.

When we reach the bottom, Star takes another path and we find ourselves scooting along the walls with our backs flat against them. It's tighter than the rest. Finally, we get to another panel and Star cracks it open just enough to listen for noises. When nothing is heard, she slides it a little more open and we squeeze through. We've come into another bedroom; one closest to the stairs.

Star raises her gun as we make our way towards the hallway. My gun is at my side but ready to go. As we turn the corner, we see movement. Darcy walks right up to the man named Vargas and stops in front of her father with tears in her eyes.

"I knew you were bad. Greedy and mean but you're more than that. Why, Daddy? Didn't you love Mom? Weren't you given the choice to be with who you wanted to be with? Why would you work so hard to take that away from Deanna, Delta and I?" she asks so softly her words are a mere whisper in the air.

"Darcy, put the gun down and let's go. Neither one of us belong here." Vernon Ramsey says and reaches for her arm. She steps back quickly and points the barrel of the shotgun at him.

"I will never go anywhere with you ever again. Do you hear me? You are dead to me. You and mom both," she yells.

"Darcy, that's enough. Let's go." he demands.

"Dad, you do not understand. Hear me!" she screams. "Levi is my reason for breathing and you are trying to have him taken from me. No more. Do you understand?" She backs away when the three men aim their handguns at her.

"Darcy, I'm not going to tell you again. Go get in my truck," he orders. She looks at the men beside her and then at Vargas.

"Please, don't hurt Levi. Please don't hurt my friends." she begs.

Vargas reaches over and caresses her cheek. "You love him. Si. I can see that, bebita. Maybe we can make a deal and your Levi won't get hurt. One that won't include your father. But as for your friends, I'm sorry, but they are all dead," he says with insane kindness.

"That's enough. Don't touch my daughter," Vernon demands and shoves Vargas.

Before I know it, all hell breaks loose as the gunmen train their sights on Vernon not Darcy. That distraction allows Darcy enough time to back away and Star to take precision shots dropping all the gunmen to the ground.

Holy shit! I had no time to react as I look around. I expect to see Vargas dead but he's gone. We hear more gunshots coming from outside. We drop to the ground and scramble for cover thinking they're for us. Star takes aim right as the front doors fly open and a team of police, some wearing uniforms, others plain clothes and some with vests marked FBI come through with their guns drawn yelling, "FBI", and spread out through the house.

Star lowers her arms and takes a deep breath. Once they clear the entry, Levi and Huck enter and head straight for Darcy and Star, asking a million questions while checking for injuries and pulling them into hugs. Two police officers come back in the foyer escorting Vernon Ramsey to the door. I watch in slow motion as his face changes to pure hate when he sees Levi consoling Darcy. He breaks free from the officer's hold and pulls a gun from inside his jacket and aims it at Levi. We all see it except for

Levi. Darcy's eyes go wide and she moves in front of Levi just as her father pulls the trigger. I watch in horror as Darcy falls back into Levi's arms and Star pulls out her gun and fires twice shooting Vernon Ramsey once in each of his legs and he drops to the ground crying out in pain.

"Darcy," I try to yell but it's only a whisper. Men rush to Darcy's father and drag him outside still screaming in pain while Levi kneels down and is talking to her, but I can't hear anything. I just want Nick. I drop to the floor and pull my legs up and curl into myself as Levi yells for help and more people rush in. My body begins shaking and my world starts going black right as I feel arms go around me and pick me up. I hear Nick's pained voice call my name as his hands run across me, searching for injuries.

CHAPTER TWENTY-TWO

I wake to the coolness of a cloth gently wiping my forehead. I open my eyes and see Nick laying next me staring down at me. When our eyes meet, he takes a deep breath and scoots down next to me and pulls me so we're chest to chest.

"You okay, baby?" he asks, his eyes searching my face. I snuggle in close to him while nodding yes but when his arms go around me, I remember and I want to tell him what how much I love him but I remember what happened.

"Darcy?" I ask.

"She's fine. The bullet just grazed her arm. Her father was aiming for Levi. Guess he pulled back at the last second. She didn't even need stitches but Vernon Ramsey isn't doing as well and Vargas got away, for now. Can't get too far in this weather. The police are out searching for him," Nick fills me in.

Out of the blue it hits me, Elvis and Buford. "Where are the dogs? I haven't seen them. Are they okay?" I ask in panic.

"The dogs are fine. They found us. We were out in the pasture trying to pull in a few strays before the clouds set in blocking out the sun. That's when the melting snow will turn to ice. Out of nowhere, those two came heading towards full speed and barking up a storm. I knew something was wrong if they were moving that fast. By the time we hit the road back here, our phones started going off. I'm so sorry, Abigail. I shouldn't have left you."

"Star, Darcy, the others, are they okay? Please tell me they're okay," I whisper.

"Everyone is okay, darlin' except for the ones Star shot and the ones the police took down outside. They're sleeping on the side of dead now. The police and FBI were headed to the Ramsey's place when Star's 911 call came in. They changed directions and came here to assist. By the time we made it here, they were already surrounding the place," he says while tugging me into his lap.

"What do you mean? How?" I ask and lay my head against his chest.

"They had agents working undercover. Been working a case against Vargas and Vernon Ramsey for a while, I guess. They've been watching and waiting, trying to draw him into the U.S. so they could arrest him. He's been able to evade them for years now. That's all they told us." he says and helps us stand. "Let's go down, check in with everyone. They've been worried about you. I want you to try and eat and then maybe we can get some sleep. We're all staying in the main house tonight at the police and FBI's request. Until they find Vargas, it'll be easier to protect us if we're all in one place. You okay with that?" he asks and I nod.

We head downstairs and when we get into the kitchen just like he said, everyone is there. There's a small bandage on Darcy's arm no bigger than a band-aid so I guess she's okay. *Thank God.* I glance around the room, taking everyone in, taking my time assuring myself everyone is okay and I see Nick talking to a woman. He gestures towards me and I watch her nod and walk to me. "Hi, I'm Delta. Darcy's sister and apparently some type of parking lot porn star," she hisses in anger.

"Oh." I study her. Seeing her sincere outrage at the accusations Ashley made against her and Nick finally reassures me one hundred percent that nothing happened that night. Relief floods me and once again, I feel light-headed. I'd almost lost him again, over a vicious lie.

"No. Nothing happened. Nick was a mess. He was an Abigail-drunk-yearning-fool all night. About the time he started singing about you, he also turned green. I reckon he was close to five beers and eight shots in. I took him outside where he promptly got sick and proceeded to half pass out. I had to be somewhere so I called Darcy. And there are no pictures because it didn't happen."

"So where have you been?" Nick questions her.

"Had some business and pleasure to take care of."

Linc comes up behind Delta and proclaims, "I'm the pleasure."

"What?" Half the room is in shock at their revelation.

"We were going to tell everyone but had to wait. Delta will explain it all in time. I will share that we are together and that Delta is going to have my baby." he gushes but Delta turns and slaps him in the chest.

"Oh, my God, you did not just blurt that out. Lincoln Jennings!" she cries out, her face red with embarrassment.

"I sure did." There's not a drop of remorse in his tone.

I can't hardly contain my grin of relief at learning the truth. Slipping my hand into Nick's, I squeeze his fingers. Staying with him, believing in him and the strength of our love had been the right decision after all.

It's getting late so everyone starts retreating to their assigned room. Nick and I say goodnight and head for the stairs, but Nick stops mid-stride.

"I have to check on the dogs. Go on up. I'll meet you there in a minute."

"Okay." I happily head to our room and once inside, walk over and sit down on the bed, relieved for this day and the drama with everything to be over when I feel something hard and cold pushed against my temple.

"Shhh, Abigail or I'll kill Nick and anyone else that walks through the door. Seems my luck is changing. Was willing to take anyone but now I have you." Vargas says against my ear. His hot, rank breath makes me feel sick and I try to pull away but he pushes the barrel to my head harder so I still. "All I need is a hostage to get me out of the country and then I'll let you go." He forcefully yanks me backwards off the bed. "I had no idea about these secret passages. Lucky for me, the police were talking about it when they walked right by me when I was hiding behind your cabin," he tells me as he drags me backwards towards another hidden panel in the room and slides it open. I fight for just a moment, but when I hear Nick and his dad coming to the room I still.

"It's up to you whether they live or die," Vargas whispers in my ear, and I can see out of the corner of my eye the barrel of a gun now aimed at the door. With that, I stop fighting and allow him to pull me behind the panel and close it. I stand behind the wall as Nick and his dad come into the room. My body is against Vargas and he still has his hand covering my mouth but lowers it slightly. "Do not speak," he warns in a silent hiss. I nod my understanding and he begins backing us further down the passageway.

Nick calls out my name in question as he opens the bathroom door. Before we get too far away I hear a panicked Nick moving about calling my name over and over. We bust through a door and the cold air hits me. I look back as it closes and see it just looks like shudder beside one of the first story windows. As I'm pulled deeper into the chilly I've had enough. I get angry and somehow break free from Vargas' and take off running.

I head towards Nick's cabin running as fast as I can, the snow crunching beneath my boots and the cold air I'm breathing in burning my throat raw. My heart is pounding as I hear footsteps behind getting closer and closer so I cut into some trees off the road to Red's place and the cabins. Once in the trees, I lose my bearings and get turned around but I don't stop running. When I come out of the trees I have no idea where I am and I slip on ice and fall on something hard. I'm stunned for a moment before I get back up. I'm now on rocks covered by the ice China warned about. I take a few careful steps, my boots slipping and sliding on the ice and I can't keep my balance. I search for anything to grab onto when I slip and fall. My body gets jostled around as it slides down a ridge. *A fucking ridge.* Where the hell did this come from? This is Texas not Arizona. Now, my only thought is, *this is how I'm going to die. Awesome.* The thought hasn't even cleared my mind when I land with a thump on a rock sticking out from the side of the ridge and my back jolts in pain.

"Umph." I groan and try to stand, but the ice is making it too slippery. I decide it's best to sit for a little while and get a plan together. Looking up, I see the top of ridge about ten feet up. Only I can't be sure, but either way I know it's too far for me to reach. The little ledge I'm on isn't wide enough for me to attempt trying to jump up and grabbing onto anything to pull myself up to the edge.

I look down to see if it's best to just drop down the rest of the way, but when I do, I see it's even worse of a drop and although the snow down there looks like a soft landing I know there could be jagged rocks. I lie back against the rocks and try to think of what to do.

It's at that moment, my mind finally picks up on the fact it's freezing out here. Above my head, at the top of the ridge, I can hear the wind and it's blowing so hard it's screaming. I roll down the sleeves of my flannel shirt over my long sleeve shirt as far as they'll go and then try to stand again. When I carefully get on my feet and steady myself I rise up on my tiptoes and let out a scream but nothing happens. My voice is still strained from yelling at Nick, the howling of the wind drowns out the minimal sound I make.

Determined, I try again, but nothing but a tiny screech escapes my mouth so I give up. I cautiously slide back down to my butt and bring my knees up and wrap my arms around myself while tucking my face into them trying to stay warm. I'm not sure how long I stay like that but eventually my skin becomes numb from the cold as darkness starts to fall. Tears try to fall down from my eyes but the little wind that is reaching me won't even allow that. My heartbreak is blown from my face by the tiny gusts of cold air. Nick calls me his fire but as the cold air sets in, my fire burns out. Soon my thoughts turn to Vargas and his threats and I get angry. I hope he gets what he deserves and more. My heart pounds hard when I remember he plans on going after my family. In a panic, I try to stand but my body won't move. It's feels like my bones are frozen. I lie my head back down and begin praying for my family's safety. Then my prayers turn to panic. No one is ever going to find me here and if they do, it won't be in time to save me from the freezing cold and in the dark setting in.

My body starts to shiver not only from the cold but also from the heartbreak of knowing I may not make it out of this. I barely my face in my arms and legs and absently start singing. *Boogie Shoes,* softly. I actually let out a half hysterical laugh. I'm becoming delirious. Singing might help distract me, so I start humming and singing everything I can think of. *I Will Survive* by Gloria Gaynor, Jason Aldean's, *She's Country*. The music is actually making me feel warmer or I'm becoming delirious. Either way, I keep singing. Soon I find myself singing, *Let It Go* by James Bay and my mood takes another turn this time for the worse as I begin thinking about Nick and how much time we wasted. Those are the last things that cross my mind, and not knowing if they'll be my last thoughts, I close my eyes.

CHAPTER TWENTY-THREE

Buford and Elvis, I'm going to miss them so much. I stir at the thought of them. I can actually hear Buford barking and I smile but then something hits me on my face and wakes me. Oh God, please don't let it be snowing. Even though I'm weak and tired I look up at the sky and see billions of stars shining brightly with an almost full moon lighting the night since the clouds having cleared from earlier today. It's beautiful. For a minute, I forget but then more snow falls on my head. I wipe the snow off as I look up. My heartbeat picks up when I see Buford looking down at me like a doggy angel. When he sees me he barks again and goes down on his front paws trying to come to me.

I put my hand out. "No, boy. Stay. Buford, stay," I order with my raspy voice. Thank God he complies before he gets hurt. He's at the top of the ridge still barking at me. "I'm okay, Buford. It's okay," I reassure him and try to stand but I can't. My bones are stiff and the rock is slippery. I collapse back onto my butt and drop my head onto my knees and hands trying to think. When I glance back up, Buford is gone. I fall back against the side of the rock, thinking I imagined him, only to feel something drop beside me. A rope is hanging down. My heart begins beating faster again and I look up and see a pair of hiking boots with spikes on the bottom start over the side and those boots are attached to a fine man in a pair of blue jeans. He's not wearing his black cowboy hat but instead a baseball cap with a light attached. It's Levi. He lowers himself beside me and smiles.

"Hey, sweetheart. So you come here often?" he asks with a smirk as he pulls a pair of gloves from his back pocket.

"My first time," I huff out a weak laugh through my relief and tears and he chuckles. I can't believe he's here. All I can do is stare at him as he gently takes my hands that are illuminated by the little bright lights that are attached to the brim of his cap by a clip. He inspects my hands and rubs them a little before slipping the gloves on them.

"So you ready to get back home?" he asks as he pulls the bottom of the rope up and makes a type of lasso and ties it around my waist and then ties it around him. He draws me in so close I can feel the heat coming off his body.

"Yes," I answer through my chattering teeth as I snuggle into him and when I do, he cusses. "I'm sorry," I mutter and pull back.

"No, honey, you're just freezing. Get in here as close as you can. Not going up yet. Just try to get a little warm. Put your hands under my coat. Warm yourself," he says and pulls my face into his neck and wraps his arms around me. He lets out a hiss when my face touches his neck.

"Sorry, again." My voice is muffled against his neck.

"No. It's okay, honey," he soothes and bends his head into me cocooning me. As I finally breathe in warm air, my lungs relax a little. I bury my face so deep into him until his long hair is covering part of my face.

"That's right, Abigail, get in here and get warm," he says gently as he rubs his hands up and down my back, arms and finally my legs.

I can feel my bones starting to warm and relax. "Hey, Levi. Isn't Texas supposed to be flat? I mean what the hell?" I ask as he continues warming me.

His deep chuckle vibrates through my body. "I think you found the only hole in the entire state of Texas, honey." he jokes. "I mean what are the odds?"

"Seems as though my odds for bad are pretty good these days." I whisper.

"Let's get you back to your man. He's going crazy," he says for the first time in seriousness and I nod wanting nothing more than that. "We're ready. Pull slowly. She's cold and hurting," he calls up.

"Got it," Linc calls back down, and slowly with Levi holding me close; we're raised back up the side of the rock.

I cry out in pain as my legs begin to straighten and hang down.

"Almost there, sweetheart. Almost there. Going to get you back home and warm. Just hold on to me," he whispers against my ear.

My God, it hurts.

When, we get to the top, Red is there too and he's leaning down telling Buford and Elvis how good they are and rubbing their heads.

CHAPTER TWENTY-FOUR

Levi pushes me up to Red by my butt and Red leans down and picks me up, cradling me close to his chest and rubbing my back as I snuggle in close to him. Linc grabs Levi's hand and pulls him up. Not waiting any longer for Levi and Linc, Red turns and heads for the trees. I hear crunching and look down and see the ice cracking as Red steps on it. He sees me looking and explains. "Spikes. Breaks up the ice," his deep voice rumbles.

"I should probably add a pair to my wardrobe," I whisper against his neck and he chuckles.

"Well, I know they're a must for my closet." Red teases and I burst out laughing shocked at this tough tattooed man joking like that. Okay, so maybe I'll be alright.

I startle when I hear a loud pop followed by a flash of light. The bright light of an orange flare lights up the Texas night sky before trailing back down, burning out only seconds before hitting the snow.

"Thank God. Is she okay? Where is she?" Nick's voice demands over the radio.

"By the ridge. She's talking and looks okay. Just meet us at the house and bring the doctor. Going straight there," Linc answers his voice calm.

"Heading there now. Tell her I love her," he says and then cuts off.

"Got it, girl?" Linc asks.

"Got it," is all I can say and lean back into Red.

We walk back through the trees with Buford and Elvis following close behind. Red stops by two ATVs and what looks like a dune buggy but I guess it's a snow buggy. They all have triangle tracks like a bulldozer, not wheels. Red sits me down in the passenger seat and grabs a bottle of water out of the backseat. He twists off the top hands before he hands it to me. "Only a couple of sips, you hear?" Red orders and I nod as a take a couple of gulps instead and hand it back to him.

Linc walks up and looks me over and then takes off his coat and begins slipping it on my arms. "I wasn't thinking you didn't have a coat. Why don't you have a coat?

If I would've have known you weren't wearing one, would've brought one. I'm sorry," he mumbles.

When he steps back, Levi comes forward with a small blanket tucks it around my hands and legs. Finally, Red pulls off his beanie and pulls it down over my head and half my eyes. I tilt my head up and look at them through my obstructed view to see them silently laughing and shaking their heads even though they still look worried. I'd fix the beanie but my hands are tucked warm beneath Levi's coat so I leave it be.

They all walk around the snow buggy and begin lowering plastic flaps and snapping them into place, blocking out some of the cold. "Elvis found me?" I ask.

"No. Elvis, she's an excellent tracker, but not too good in snow. Buford found you. He led us right to you," Levi explains.

I look over at the dogs and my heart warms and tears fill my eyes. "You two are getting some serious doggy treats first chance. Like gobs and gobs of doggy treats. Thank you." They make their way through the snow to me. I pull my hands from the blanket and rub them for only a second because I'm just too tired and weak.

"Alright, Elvis and Buford. We got her. Y'all did real good," Levi praises them. "Get on back home." Both dogs obey and take off through the snow heading back home.

Once Red's in the driver's seat, he grins again before turning serious and tucking my hands back in under the blanket. "You okay, sugar? Looks like you might have some windburn. Anything else hurt?" he asks while gently turning my face.

"No, I mean I may have some scrapes, but mostly my skin is coming back alive and it burns," I answer.

The ATV starts up and I try looking around but my vision is still blocked from the beanie. Red notices and reaches over and flips the front up a little so I can see.

"Thanks," I say softly.

"Let's get you back. I think your parents are close to arriving."

"What?" I blurt out as my breathing becomes heavy.

"Yeah, sugar, Nick called your mom and dad when we couldn't find you and they started up. They might even be there by the time we get back."

As we make our way back to the house, I try watching my surroundings and I want to ask Red if they caught Vargas but I can barely keep my eyes open and start to panic at how lethargic I feel. I kick off the blanket trying to stay awake and turn to Red. "Why am I so tired?" I ask in alarm and reach for the snap on the plastic guard to open it and let air in. I can't breathe. I can't get a good breath.

Red stops the snow buggy and leans in and gently grabs my hands and pulls them down before pulling my face up to his.

"You're crashing, Abigail but you're okay. You've been surviving on adrenaline and now that it's over and your mind knows you're safe, it's giving your body permission to shut down and get the sleep you need. I promise, I'll get you back safe. Close your eyes and rest. It's going to take almost an hour to get you back because of the snow drifts the wind kicked up. Just take a little nap," his gentle voice reassures me.

I lean back in my seat as he repositions the blanket over my legs.

"You okay? You ready?" he asks gently and as my eyes become even heavier I give a sight nod.

Linc and Levi pull up next to us and Levi calls out, "She okay?"

"She's crashing and trying to fight it. Small panic attack but she's okay now. Let's go." Red calls back.

I take calming breaths as I visualize my mom and dad. I feel like I'm five years old and all I want is my mommy and daddy. I try to control my crying but I know the dam is going to break as soon as I see them.

CHAPTER TWENTY-FIVE

I must fall asleep because I only wake when I feel my body being picked up and cradled against a big warm chest. I know the feel of this chest and the smell of this man because he's been carrying me like this since I was a baby. It's my dad.

I'm too weak to do more than whisper, "Daddy?" before beginning to cry.

"Abigail, baby girl." His pained voice whispers back.

He walks with me in his arms up the steps. "Is she okay?" my mom's voice is laced with worry.

"I don't know," my dad tells her.

"In here." *Nick.* He's here.

My dad gently places me on a bed. I'm so tired. The warmth of the inside keeps me in a deep slumber-like state and I can't even speak. I try to call out for Nick and he must hear me because then he's right beside me.

"I'm here, fire." he whispers against my lips as he kisses me softly and caresses my cheeks.

CHAPTER TWENTY-SIX

I feel my clothes being taken from my body starting with my socks and boots. I don't know who's doing it and I don't even care except for when they start pulling my jeans down my legs. It burns a little and I let out a soft whimper.

"I'm sorry, honey. So sorry," my mom's voice is full of anguish.

I whimper again when they begin pulling my shirt off and I hear a voice that shocks me and my body shakes with a sob.

"I got you, baby sissy. Let me get this off and then it'll be okay. Take a few breaths, close your eyes and when you're ready hold your breath. Like the time I had to pull the broken glass from your foot. Remember? Hold your breath and close your eyes. Let me know when," Jaycee says softly.

When Jaycee and I were kids we were always off and exploring up at the lake in the hill country. One day when I was about seven and Jaycee ten years old, we came across a sandy area not too far from a beach. We took off our flip flops and were playing in the sand but when we got up to leave I stepped on a piece of broken glass hidden in the sand and started to cry. It was just Jaycee and I and we didn't know what to do. I was too big for her to carry and I was too scared to let her leave me alone and go for help. I couldn't walk on it without causing the glass to go further into my foot so after Jaycee calmed me, she had me close my eyes and hold my breath while she pulled the glass out of my foot quickly.

"I got you, baby sissy. Close your eyes and keep them closed until I tell you to open them. Now, hold your breath."

After Jaycee pulled the shard of glass from my foot she helped me limp back to where our parents and grandparents were and they cleaned and bandaged my foot.

I take a few breaths and nod my head before holding my breath as my mom and Jaycee pull the final clothes from my body.

"Here," a voice I recognize as China's says to someone and then warmth surrounds me. Someone is wrapping me in the softest heated blankets. I'm tucked in tight from my shoulder to my toes. It's Jaycee. It's the same way she tucks in Callie at bedtime. As I think of Callie, I smile and fall back asleep.

CHAPTER TWENTY-SEVEN

I hear a man's voice calling me and I open my eyes. An older man with gray hair and a moustache is sitting next to me on the bed and Nick and my dad are standing behind him. He begins to pull the blankets from my body and I can't help but whimper when I feel the cool air.

"Abigail, what's wrong?" he asks.

"It's cold." I complain.

"It's okay. I'm not going to lift it again right now. Hold on." he tells me.

"She has a mild case of windburn. It's similar to sunburn and her skin might have a tingling sensation for the next few hours but she'll be fine. Falling down in the ridge and being stuck on that ledge actually protected her from the winds above. I expected much worse when China called and told me she'd been out in this weather for almost four hours before you found her."

Four hours? I think to myself. And then not even four? Almost four? Seemed much longer. Maybe they're wrong or I crossed into the Pacific Time zone because it felt like an eternity. As the doctor goes on, I decide being alive is what's important even though they are clearly mistaken. Instead of pointing that out to them I listen to him as he continues talking to Nick. But only four hours? Really?

"She might not be here otherwise. She's one blessed girl. Between the weather and falling down into that ridge and landing on the little ledge, someone was watching out for her. 'Bout that area it drops down about thirty feet. She was smart waiting and not trying to climb up," he tells them.

thirty-foot ridge. Oh, my God! I thought maybe twenty but I knew there would be rocks. I just didn't realize the snow was that deep. Jesus, thank you, I send my thanks up to God.

"I have some oil that will help with the burn. I'll leave a bottle. Her skin might peel and itch a little. I'll give her an inflammatory medicine which will help. Have her use an aloe based lotion for a few days. Use the oil as needed the first few days and the lotion after, at least twice a day and no hot showers and absolutely no soaking in hot

198

baths even though I know she'll want that. Going to also give her something to help her soreness from the fall. Red said she complained about her back hurting from her hard landing. She'll be feeling pain from that most. I'll throw in some Vicodin to cover the first few days when the discomfort will be its worse. Make sure she eats before taking it. Most important, the shock to her body. She's needs rest and no more excitement," he instructs my dad and Nick before turning to me.

"Hey there, Abigail. I'm Dr. Santos. You allergic to anything you know of?" he asks and I shake my head. "Do you remember what happened?" He helps me up into a sitting position and I nod as I shiver from losing the warmth at my back. "I'm going to need to check you over real quick and then I want to get some warm tea in you. Do you have a favorite?" I shake my head, no.

Dr. Santos pulls a stethoscope from his bag and hooks the ear pieces in his ears. "Going to take a listen, okay?" he says and rubs the chest piece of the stethoscope on his jeaned thigh, warming it. He feels it was his palm before he lowers the blanket down just enough to place it over my heart. "I know it's still a little cold. Sorry. I'm sure you've had enough cold to last you a good bit, huh?" he asks while moving it around to my back. "Take a few deep breaths for me," he instructs.

I begin taking deep breaths and I lock gazes with Nick. He's scared to death; I can tell but he gives me a smile. I smile back as best I can as the doctor lowers me back down to the bed.

"Sounds good," Dr. Santos tells us as he drops his stethoscope back into his bag, "I need to uncover you a bit and do an exam but I'll be quick so you can get back under your blanket. You okay with who's in here?" he calls from the bathroom where's he's washing his hands.

I look at my dad and he throws up his hands and gives me a sad grin. "Got it," he says and turns for the door. "You want your mom or Jaycee?" he asks.

"Jaycee," I call out hoarsely, my voice dry.

"I'll get her." The doctor comes back in and is drying his hands when we both glance at Nick. He takes the hint too and leaves after giving me a soft kiss on the lips.

"I'll get you some tea," he says and then follows my dad out. Before he can close the door, Jaycee walks in and sits on the opposite side of the bed.

Dr. Santos checks my reflexes, ears, nose and throat and after putting a thermometer in my mouth, begins turning me, checking my skin while prodding and poking me.

"It's not too bad at all. I've seen much worse. Before I go, I'm going to give you a steroid shot and a valium. I need you to rest. But first, let's have your sister here help you rinse off in the shower. You have a few scrapes on your lower back and thighs and there's gravel imbedded in your skin. I need you to gently spray the area, not wash it, and try to dislodge what you can. Don't want that area getting more inflamed and irritated or infected. Do not try to use hot water; it'll burn even though your skin isn't too bad. Use very lukewarm or cool water. Make it the coolest you can tolerate. The cooler the water the better. It'll also help pull what little burn you have from your skin, but no longer than three minutes. Make that a rule for the next few days. I'll leave oil for you to rub on after you get out of the shower and try to get it everywhere. If you have a robe or a big towel, wear it but no tight clothing for a few hours. While you do that, I'm going to write out your prescriptions and take them down to your family so they can run into town and get them filled. When you're done with your shower, send your sister down and I'll come back up and we can finish up," he orders, tapping my leg before grabbing his bag and walking out of the room.

Jaycee stands and looks around the room. She opens the door to the bathroom and steps inside. Soon I hear the water of the shower running so I scoot to the edge of the bed, stand and make my way to the bathroom feeling weak and sore.

"You okay?" Jaycee asks. She pulls down a towel from the shelf and sets it on the toilet and reaches in and tests the water

"I was all wrong about Nick but in my defense, so was he. That bitch Ashley was actually trying to blackmail him or something." I blurt out before carefully stepping in the shower. I shiver under the cool water. Jaycee gasps. "What?" She pulls the shower curtain back enough to peek in. I tell what I found out as best I aim my sore back towards the spray. Before too long I'm just too tired to stay in any longer and turn off the water. I reach for the towel, wrapping it around me as I take a seat on the toilet. Jaycee grabs another towel and starts drying my hair. I hear Jaycee mutter insults that make no sense under her breath and I actually smile.

"Then why did you take off? I thought you and Nick had a fight."

"What?" Don't they know? "Vargas. I was going to sleep when he grabbed me from behind."

"What?" Nick's menacing tone comes from the doorway.

"He came in through the hidden passages. He took me but I got away and ran. I thought you knew."

The atmosphere in the room has changed. Buford and Elvis are both standing and waiting to be told what to do. I turn fully towards him and see him with the phone to his ear.

"Get up here now," he says and pulls a gun from the back of jeans.

"Darlin', are you saying Vargas was in this house and that's why you left? He took you?" he asks through a hiss. "He's the reason you're hurt?" He gently covers my body with the towel as I nod yes. "I didn't know that. Thought you were mad or walked off and got yourself lost or something but no, no one knew that," he informs me. There's there's a knock at the door and Levi and Huck enter.

"I'm sorry," I whisper, exhaustion causing tears to spring to my eyes.

"Darlin', it's not your fault. That bastard came into this house and took you and he's going to pay," he promises as Dr. Santos and Delta come into the room.

Huck hears him. What the fuck are you talking about?"

"Vargas. He came in through the passageways and took her. He could be in here right fucking now," he barks at Huck and Levi. "He came for her and now that Jaycee is here, he'll go for her too. Get everyone together. We need to get behind these walls and make sure he's not here," he growls. "Don't worry about capturing the fucker, just kill him. Darlin', I need to go but I want you to stay here and rest," Nick says and for the first time I actually feel a terrifying level of fear take over my emotions. Fear for Nick.

Dr. Santos steps forward as tears roll from my eyes and into my damp hair, some falling onto the pillow. "Go, I'm going to give her a shot that'll keep her out for a while. She doesn't need any more excitement. It could actually cause her harm," he says and pulls out a syringe.

"Wait. What if he's here and comes for me again? How can I protect myself if I'm knocked out?" I ask, starting to panic again.

"I'll stay with you." Delta offers.

Dr. Santos leans down and lifts my towel just enough to reach my hip and within seconds I feel a burn spread through my body and my eyes begin to droop.

Nick leans down and kisses my lips as the doctor gives me a second shot.

"I'll be back. I promise. Delta is going to stay with you. She'll watch out for you and Buford and Elvis are on alert and won't leave your side. I love you." He kisses me softly again before backing away.

"I love you too, Nick." I whisper.

Nick brings his face only a breath away from mine.

I manage to raise my arms enough to wrap them around his neck and pull him back to me. "I love you, honeysuckle," I whisper, "and when I'm better, I going to kick Ashley's ass." I say and let him go.

He chuckles and then Delta chimes in. "And I'll be getting in on that action."

CHAPTER TWENTY-EIGHT

I've been awake for a couple hours and Elvis and Buford haven't left my side. Jaycee, Star, Darcy and Delta have been talking and Delta told me nothing happened between her and Nick that night. Like Darcy, she thinks of Nick as a brother and that would just be too gross. She did remember seeing Ashley and her brood of bitches watching them and at one point Ashley began to approach them. That's when she decided to take Nick outside and call Darcy. I want to talk to Nick some more but he's not back yet. They're still out looking for Vargas and we've been told to just sit tight. Star and Delta are both armed and ready for just about anything. There's a knock at the door and China enters, her eyes aimed dead on at Delta.

"Delta, oh, I'm sorry," she says sarcastically and throws her arms in the air. "I mean FBI, Special Agent Ramsey." China puts her hands on her hips and frowns at her. "There's a Major Peters here from the DEA and he needs to speak with you," her tone conveying her anger.

"And when he's done, young lady, I'll need to speak with you. Come on, Buford and Elvis, y'all need to go out for a while," she commands, and the dogs follow her out of the room.

Delta smiles at us, taking no notice of our dropped jaws and bewildered stares. "I can explain, and I will. I need to talk to Peters first and then apparently get my ass chewed out by China like I'm ten years old and not pushing thirty-one," she mumbles as she leaves the room.

No one has mentioned Vernon Ramsey but I'm sure what has happened is weighing heavy on Delta and Darcy's mind as well as Star who shot him.

"Oh hell no, I'm not waiting up here. I want to see this," Star announces and hops up from my bed where she'd been laying with me.

"Me too," Darcy agrees.

As they start for the door I yell out, "Wait. Me three." I jump off the bed, sway for a minute from the effects of the valium, and then steady myself. We head down the hallway for the stairs with Darcy and Star each holding on to me in case I take a nosedive from the medication.

Stopping at the railing of the balcony that sits on the second floor, we are just in time to observe half dozen agents enter the house carrying a cold and shivering Vargas. His head is hung down, that is until he hears a voice and then it snaps up and he snarls at the man wearing an FBI vest standing across from him.

CHAPTER TWENTY-NINE

"Hermano," the agent says and Vargas spits at him.

"You're not my brother. You are a pig and trader," he growls and tries to lunge for the agent.

"You're right. You're not my brother, Andres. You're a murderer, a low-life drug dealer and when you drugged unwilling people, tortured and experimented on the innocents, you violated their human rights. The UN wants you and the others punished and made an example of which many are standing in line to make happen. You're now nothing and you have nothing," the agent says before stepping up so that he's only a couple of feet from Vargas.

"Oh really?" Vargas laughs nervously. "My lawyers will fight the UN on all these charges. You can't prove anything and Mexico will welcome me home like always. Nothing will change, Santino," he says through gritted teeth as he leans in.

"Everything has changed, Hermano. Everything. As we speak, your crops are being extracted. Drug routes destroyed. Your men arrested and the ones you kept as slaves are now free and being paid to remove and destroy your fields' compliments of the U.S. They're doing it with smiles on their faces and because I asked my bosses nicely, they've allowed me to oversee the destruction of your home. You won't need it where you're going. Oh, and after all your filth is removed from God's soil, your land will be donated to the local towns for farming legitimate crops. The ones you tortured with threats for over a decade are rejoicing. There will be no welcome home for you. You have nothing left. Your wife, Catalina, the only one who stayed all these years out of fear is on a plane; ready to start a new life, a life free of you. You. Are. Done!" he barks at Vargas.

Vargas' face has turned red and just when I think it can't get any more intense Vargas sees something, someone has come up and is standing behind Santino. He freezes and his eyes go wide as he lets out a string of Spanish curses and starts trying to free himself from the agents holding him. I can't see the face of the person standing behind Santino but I can see part of his FBI vest. We watch as the man says something to Vargas that sets him off again.

"He killed mi hijo! He killed your nephew and you stand with him like *he's* your hermano?" Vargas spits.

"My nephew was trash and did not deserve to breathe, just like his father, he was a monster. One just like you. Yes, he killed your son. He killed him when he walked in on him beating and trying to rape a child. He is more of my brother than you ever were or will be," Santino says in a low, dangerous voice and takes another step forward.

Everyone in the room goes on alert when he leans in and looks in his brother in the eyes and puts his hand on his gun. A man in a suit tries to snap him out of his haze of anger, by placing a restraining hand on his shoulder, but Santino doesn't flinch. His eyes bore into Vargas'. "Do you know who that child was? The thirteen-year-old girl? The one your son was trying to rape?" He doesn't wait for an answer. "Quien era su sobrina, mi hija," he says, his voice tortured.

Vargas head snaps back and again he tries to jerk from the agents hold. "Mentiras!" he screams.

"No, no, no, no, brother. I walked in after him and Alanza was beaten, bleeding and her clothes ripped. Sombra saved her," he informs him and stands back at his full height. "I'm done. Take him," Santino orders.

I follow Santino's path with my eyes long enough that they catch on someone else. My eyes travel up the agent's chest and arms that are partly covered in tattoos. I briefly stop on his chest where it says FBI and then I notice the tattoo on his neck, *Sombra*.

"Shadow." I whisper. When my eyes reach his, I lose my breath. He only looks at me briefly before bowing his head and walking away in the same direction as Santino. No way. I'm panicked for Jaycee but when I look over at her she doesn't look frightened. "You know?" I ask, shocked.

"I'll explain later. Let's go find our men. What do you say, girls?" she asks completely calm.

"A lot of people have a lot of explaining to do later," I say to myself as I start down the stairs.

I only make it halfway down before Nick comes around the corner with Blue. Despite everything, my face lights up when I see him.

"Blue!" I yell and hurry down the stairs faster than I should, only to trip and fall. Luckily, Nick anticipates my clumsiness and rushes up and catches me before gently standing me back up. I'm about to say thank you when an angry voice bellows.

"Jesus, Abigail Caoimhe McGinty, slow down. You're hurt for Christ's sake." I grin, knowing it's my dad. It's been a tough day so I decide not to poke the bear.

"Sorry, Dad but it's Blue." I tell him.

"Hell's creek, these girls are going to get me locked up," he says in irritation. "Well, hell, Blue, go give her a goddamn hug before she kills herself, but be careful," he barks at Blue and a chorus of chuckles and giggles echo from the other room. "I need a damn drink," my dad says to himself.

Ronan must hear him because approaches my dad. "You're not the only one. Let's hit my stash of whiskey," he suggests. I can't help but laugh as I watch them go.

"Our poor dad's." I say to Nick and he laughs. "And they ain't see nothing yet." I say and glance at Jaycee.

"Good Lord." This from my mom, Violet. On cue, China walks in.

"Violet I also have a stash. Would you like to down a bottle of wine with me?" China asks as she heads back into the kitchen. My mom turns around and points at Jaycee and I.

"Behave you two." she orders.

Nick and I laugh as Blue finally makes it to me and pulls me into a soft hug. He whispers in my ear. "You scared me, Abigail." He squeezes me a little tighter before letting me go.

"I'm sorry," I say and kiss his cheek. A low growl escapes from Nick at our contact and I look up at him. "What, he's like my brother," I say in defense.

"But he's not," he counters, drawing me closer to him.

"Almost," I try and reason again.

"Not even close."

Jaycee and Blue start laughing and join in with a giggle before winking at Blue.

"Darlin', you're supposed to be resting. Let's get you back at bed," Nick says while gently touching my face. "I need to rub more oil on you and you have to take your medicine."

I know he's right so I turn to Blue and Jaycee. "Y'all will be here in the morning right?" I practically beg.

Blue laughs. "We're staying for a couple of days and then heading back," he informs me, smiling at my relieved expression

"We're staying across the hall from you. I'll be here if you need me, baby sissy, but for now he's right, get some rest. I'm going down to the kitchen and I'll get y'all something to eat. Y'all can hang out in there and talk," she suggests and her and Blue start down the stairs and Nick and I return to our room.

CHAPTER THIRTY

In our room, I head for the bed as Nick picks up a bag of medicine sitting on the dresser. "Red and Lina ran into town and got these for you," he says with his back to me while pulling out the bottles one by one and reading them.

"So did Lina and Linc get to see Rocky?" I ask, taking a chance. Nick turns around slowly and looks at me but doesn't say anything. "I saw him. I know he's alive," I tell him, tilting my head.

"Yes, they did," he says and walks over to me holding one of the bottles. "Abigail from what Linc told me, he's not Rocky or Daniel anymore. He's working with the FBI, taking on assignments no one else wants from what I understand. He's only back for right now because of this case. Vernon Ramsey's involvement with Vargas is what brought him to town," Nick explains as he sets the pills down on the nightstand. "You need to eat first. We'll wait till Jaycee brings you food. How's your pain?" he asks as he picks up the oil and squats down in front of me, pours some of on his hands and starts rubbing it on my calves.

"Doesn't hurt as bad as I thought it would at all. Just little tingles now and then. Kind of itchy is all. It's my bones that ache a little," I tell him then moan as his hands start to massage the aches from my legs. "God, that feels good, baby," I say and close my eyes in bliss. Nick groans and l open my eyes to find his stare locked on me.

"Fuck, Abigail, don't do that," he says while pouring more oil on his hands. "Give me your arms," he says and reaches for one.

"But you didn't finish my legs, Nick," I tease him as I lift my leg and rest my foot against his chest.

He eyes travel up my leg and he looks at me from under his eyes lashes as his hands go back to massaging my calf. "You want me to finish your legs, darlin'?" he asks as he runs his hands up my thigh and to my tummy causing me to lie back on the bed. "You want me to oil anything else up?" he asks as both his hands travel back down my legs. On their way back up, his thumbs touch me and I moan and raise my hips.

"Fuck," Nick breathes and then he's up and locking the door. He unties my robe and pulls the sides open, leaving me exposed. My breathing escalates as he grabs the oil again and starts rubbing it on my stomach and finally my breasts. I push up into his hands as he squeezes my mounds before teasing the nipples and pinching them. "You like that?" he asks as his hands go back down and gently pull my legs apart. I barely get out a yes as he touches and starts to circle me. I moan and squirm, needing more.

"More please," I beg softly. He keeps circling me and brings his other hand down and enters me with his fingers. He moves them in and out but it's not enough. I need him. I reach up and grab for his belt but he stops me.

"No. This is for you. Don't want to hurt you," he says and starts circling me again.

"Nick. I need you inside me. Please?" I beg and rise up but he stops me again.

"I don't want to hurt you," he repeats as he undoes his belt. I squirm around waiting for him to be inside me. I keep my eyes on his hands as he lowers his jeans enough to set himself free. "Stay just like that," he orders and pulls my hips closer to the edge of the mattress. I let my legs fall apart and when I do, he growls while looking down at me. He pumps himself a few times before putting himself at my entrance. When he starts in, he stands to his full height and begins slowly thrusting in me while only touching my knees. I lower my hand and start circling myself and when he sees me touching myself, gentle turns into deep and hard thrusts. He keeps watching my hand while licking and biting his lip.

"Fuck, that's hot," he says and I clench around him. He feels it and picks up his speed. I bring my other hand to my nipple and start pinching it the way he did only a little harder. I'm so close and I start to push back into him. "I'm there, darlin'. I can feel you. Go. Don't hold back," he orders as he hooks his hands under my knees and lifts my hips so he can go deeper. That's all it takes and I explode, Nick following me seconds later. He pulls out of me and then undoes his pants while grinning down at me. He walks into the bathroom and wets a cloth with warm water and cleans me before closing up my robe. I scoot back on the bed and lay down while he tosses the towel back in the bathroom hamper. I can't help the grin on my face but then I remember being on the ledge and almost letting go of him, of us. Thinking I had nothing to come back to. He rejoins me as a couple of tears slide out of my eyes.

"Nick," I sob. "I'm sorry. I love you." Before the words are out of my mouth, he's lying next to me and pulling me into his arms.

"What's wrong? Did I hurt you?" he asks, worried. I shake my head as I scoot closer. "What is it then?" he presses.

"I almost lost you again. I almost let go," I whimper through my pain and look away in regret.

"Fire, did you really think I was going to let you leave me again?" He asks pulling my face back at his. "Worst case scenario and everything we thought happened did happen, I still would have fought for you and I would have won. I'm not letting you go, ever, and you'll never have to worry again," he reassures me, leaning in for a kiss.

"I love you, Nick. So much," I moan against his lips.

"Love you too, Abigail."

We lay on our sides, nothing touching but our lips and tongues until we hear a soft knock on the door. Nick pulls away and smiles as he gets up and opens the door. Jaycee, Blue, Linc, Delta, Levi, Darcy and then Star and Huck enter carrying pizzas and paper plates. I sit up and smile and clap when I see the boxes and Jaycee starts laughing.

"Pizza!" I cry out in excitement.

Nick takes the pizzas and spreads them out across the room. Everyone grabs a plate and starts loading up and eating while Nick makes me a plate and sits next to me on the bed while Jaycee and the girls pile on the end. The men take the chairs and lean against the wall and we all dig in.

"Wait," Star says and hops off the bed and heads down the hall. She comes back carrying an armful of cherry cokes for everyone. She hands them out, but the guys all shake their head.

Finally, Levi speaks up. "I don't know how you can drink that stuff. It's disgusting." He makes a face around his bite of pizza. The guys all give a shout out telling him they agree.

Nick hops off the bed and goes over to a picture on the wall and opens it. My mouth drops when I realize it's on hinges. He reaches in and pulls out beers as the guys' line up taking one from him.

"What the hell?" Star demands.

"This one was ours," Huck says, laughing.

"I've slept in this room and I had no clue," Darcy chimes in.

"You remember that night, the time when we all stayed over because of the thunderstorm? It was just a few months after I moved to town." He smirks and Darcy grins at the memory.

"The first night you kissed me," she recollects with a blush.

"Yes, the first night we made out," he teases and she blushes even more.

Huck and Nick laugh as they both call him an asshole.

"Nick said he had beer stashed in here and they dared me to sneak in while you were sleeping and grab some. Said the girls didn't know about this spot and under no circumstances were y'all to find out. I agreed to take on the mission. Willing to die for the cause and not let the brotherhood down. Failure was not an option," he says and everyone in the room laughs.

"No way," Darcy scoffs.

"Yes," he tells her. "It's true. I came in and searched the room looking for the right picture when I heard you stir because freaking Huck fell down outside the door and cussed." Levi recounts, shooting Huck a glare.

"I fell over Nick, when he stopped for nothing," Huck complains.

"Thought I heard something," Nick says in defense.

"Don't care," Levi tells them. "Anyway, I froze thinking you woke up but when you didn't move again I checked to make sure you were still asleep. When I saw you, I couldn't take my eyes off you. You were so beautiful and I just stood there watching you sleep." His eyes go soft as he makes his admission.

"Creep!" Huck calls out and without taking his eyes from Darcy, Levy raises his hand and gives Huck 'the bird'.

"You must have sensed me because you opened your eyes and when you saw me watching you, you didn't scream, you smiled," he says softly but it's almost a question.

"I thought I was dreaming. It was the best dream ever," she tells him as her eyes turn glassy.

"I don't know why but I had to kiss you," he admits and leans in and kisses her again.

"Yeah and the asshole stayed in here all damn night and never came back with the beer," Nick complains.

"Nope," Levi says as he deepens the kiss between him and Darcy.

Nick winks at me and I have a feeling there was more to that mission than just beer. Levi breaks the kiss but keeps his eyes on Darcy.

"That was a long time ago. Almost fourteen years ago. Think it's time to make it official, babe," Levi says. "I keep waiting for the right time and I think right now is it. Our obstacles' are gone." He reaches into his pocket and pulls out a ring.

I think we all know that obstacle was Vernon Ramsey. The fact that no one is too torn up about what happened to Vernon is a horrible testament to what an evil man he must be.

All the women lean forward to get a look at the ring. It's incredible. It's a silver band with turquoise around the band and a princess cut diamond. I've never seen anything like it.

"Levi no that was your mom's," she whispers as tears start trailing down her cheeks.

"Yes." His own eyes become glassy. "I'm doing this and I'm doing it now," he tells her and gets down on one knee

I briefly look around the room to see all the women have locked onto their men and everyone is watching with love.

"When Ina was sick she called me to her one night. She gave me her ring and told me she wanted you to have it. Said to stop wasting time and to marry you. Look inside, read it," he tells her and hands it to her.

Darcy takes it, her hands shaking and as reads the inscription, she hiccups a sob.

"My mother and father lived and loved by these words. It's hung in a small frame in our living room. Do you remember?" he asks and Darcy nods.

"Love me without fear. Trust me without questions. Need me without demanding. Want me without restrictions. Accept me without change. Desire me without inhibitions," he recites.

"For a love so free will never fly away," Darcy says through her tears.

"She said it was her blessing. She told me her love for my father was love eternal and would live on in the Spirit World. She didn't know he'd be following her there soon," Levi says and Darcy cups his cheek.

"I'm sorry, Levi," she whispers.

He kisses her hand and then goes on. "Their love was so strong it's crossed worlds but it also bound them and they needed to be together. I understand that love because our love is the same. She said she was leaving some of her love here with us. This ring carries her love, their love. She said the spirit of their love would live in it and combined with ours would make us unbreakable." He takes the ring back before clasping her hands in his. "Darcy, you are my chante, my heart. I love you and have since the night I walked in here and kissed you. Will you please do me the honor of being my wife?" he asks as he looks in her eyes.

Darcy doesn't hesitate. "Yes," she answers and jumps into his arms.

Levi doesn't wait. He picks her up and heads out of the room, "We're out!" he calls over his shoulder and everyone laughs.

"Oh, my God, that was beautiful," Star says and snuggles into Huck.

"Yeah, it was." Huck kisses Star on the head. "You ready for bed, honey?" he asks. When Star says yes he takes her hand and leads her out of the room.

"We're out too," Linc says and wraps his arm around Delta's shoulders. "Got to get back and check on some stuff but should be here in the morning for breakfast," he says as Delta starts closing up the boxes of pizza and stacking them.

"I'll take these down. Warning for you two," she points at Jaycee and me, "China, Lina and your Mom are downstairs and just opened their fourth bottle of wine. They plan on dragging us all into town tomorrow to go Christmas shopping. Just giving you a heads up," she warns us and hands the pizza boxes to Linc. "Won't be too early though. I think they'll be sleeping in and then needing some aspirin before any big time shopping quests." She laughs and leaves the room but stops when Blue speaks up.

"How is he?" he asks, his tone somber.

"Don't understand, after all that happened." Linc shakes his head. "I'm his brother; it's easier for me, but y'all?" He stares at Blue and Jaycee in awe.

"It's taken some time, but Jaycee's teaching me about forgiveness and moving forward. Plus, it's not his fault. That's the part I struggled with. It was him but not him. I think I finally gave up trying to make everything fit. Jaycee told me to turn it over to God and he would give me peace. I prayed and let it go as much as I can." He grasps Jaycee's hand. "And I found some peace," he tells Linc. "If she can forgive him..." His words stop there and he leaves the rest for us.

We all know Jaycee went through more than what was told to us but that's something she's decided to keep between Blue, Rocky and herself. My sissy is a rare light, always believing and seeing the good in people. I used to wonder if she was too innocent because of the way she grew up protected by the men around us, but it's actually the opposite. I think they all taught and instilled her with inner iron strength. One that allows her to forgive on a higher level than the rest us. Slowly, she's teaching us, showing us through her actions of forgiveness and not looking back at things with bitterness. She's never felt sorry for herself or questioned why, especially when it came to Rocky.

"I don't ask why because I know one day He will show me why. I have faith in Him, baby sissy." Is how she'd

228

explained it to me. Soon the anger and pain I was keeping began to subside and my heart lightened. I'm not where Jaycee is, but one day I hope to give Rocky my complete forgiveness even though I know he himself doesn't believe he deserves it. Whether he does or doesn't, I'm learning it's not for me to decide.

"Hate the sin, not the sinner, sweet Abigail; it saves us a lot of grief and confusion of the heart." My grandma had told me that one night, and it has stuck in the back of my mind ever since; something about those words just clicked in my head and heart. Catching the glimpse of Rocky earlier, I know without anyone telling me he's exactly opposite of the guy at the dance hall. That guy was clean-cut, no tattoos and the son of a doctor. That guy hurt people as a result of his father's greed. This new man had long hair, a beard and was covered in tattoos. He's reinvented himself or gone through a rebirth.

"He's better. He's working with the FBI and other agencies. They're helping him. Have him seeing doctors and getting treatment. He's determined to live in the shadows though. Breaks my heart and my mom's." Linc shrugs his shoulders. "I'm just glad he's here if only for a little while. I'll take what I can get," he tells us and looks at Delta. "She's resigning now that she's having my baby. Met her a few

229

weeks back. Came into town with Daniel and Santino. She'd been working her dad, getting information while Daniel and Santino worked the darker part of the assignment. Just glad it's over." He pulls her close and starts back out the door.

"Sorry about your dad," I call out, my voice full of sadness for her and Darcy.

"Don't be. He wouldn't have been sorry if it were any of you. My mom, she's already playing innocent but I was there and I know she's not. She's has her own set of charges she'll be dealing with and she'll pay too. One way or another they're both going to pay for their dirty deeds. I'll make sure of it," Darcy replies.

"Linc! Hang on!" Jaycee yells. She runs across the hall to her room, coming back a few minutes later and handing Linc a small jewelry box. "Sorry, but please give this to him. Tell him to give it to her himself."

Linc nods and examines the box. "Do you mind?" he asks. Jaycee smiles and gives a little nod, granting him permission. He opens it, pulls out a small pouch and turns it upside down letting the contents fall into the palm of his hand. When he sees it, he looks surprised. "I don't believe it," he whispers. "If it's not the same one but it's almost identical." He runs his finger over it before placing it back in the pouch, closing the box and putting it in his pocket.

"What is it?" Delta inquires.

Lincoln smiles at all of us before answering. "Did he ever tell you about our mamo?" He asks. Darcy shakes her head. "Our grandmother, our dad's mom, she was the sweetest woman you'd ever want to meet. Not a mean bone in her body and when she was alive, my dad was a different person. She passed when Daniel and I were still young. I remember Daniel would always play with her necklace when she held him. She'd ask, "You like that, Danny boy? I'll give it to you one day and you can give it to your special girl." When she died, she did what she promised and left it for him. Later, when Daniel asked for it, my dad told him he didn't know where it went. This can't be the same one but its pretty close." Linc lowers his head and Delta steps closer to him and rises up on her tiptoes and gives him a soft kiss. "I'm so glad he remembered her and that memory. Means he's still in there. He's just got to fight to find his way back," Linc says and leaves the room. Delta gives us a small smile and before following him.

Okay, that was emotional.

"Okay, let's get going, love," Blue tells Jaycee.

Jaycee starts to pout but Blue leans in and kisses her. "Come on, you won't be pouting for long," he teases and Jaycee blushes.

"You okay?" she asks me.

"Yes, I'm fine. Go do the nasty with your man, tramp," I tease and Nick and I start laughing.

"Jesus Christ," Blue mutters. Jaycee gives me a final wave before he closes the door.

Nick locks our door before securing the windows and pushing a large chair in front of the panel that Vargas came in through. When he turns back, I raise an eyebrow at him.

"After all those stories, I don't trust anyone not to sneak in here while we're sleeping," he explains as he undresses. "You need anything?" he asks as he heads to the bathroom and pulls out his toothbrush and toothpaste. I slide off the bed and walk over to stand next to him.

"I need to brush my teeth too," I say and his eyes crinkle up while he finishes up brushing his teeth.

"Wouldn't have it any other way," he says as he cleans off his toothbrush and hands it to me. I smile as I load the toothbrush but gasp when I look in the mirror and see my hair and face.

"Oh, my God! Why didn't you tell me, Nick?" I squeal before I finish up brushing my teeth, now angry. "Lord, everyone saw me like this?" I say to myself and start looking around for a hairbrush. "I need a hairbrush," I cry out. "Why didn't you tell me my hair looked like a bird's nest, Nick? I need a brush!" I demand, almost in a yell.

I walk back into the bedroom and start searching for a hairbrush when there's a knock on the door. Nick's got nothing on but his boxers. "You're closer," he says. "And dressed," he laughs when I try to straighten my hair.

"Nick!" I whine and then decide what the hell. Everyone's already seen me. I open the door and there stands a shirtless Blue. *Okay, wow.* My sister is one lucky girl. When I decide to quit ogling his beautiful chest, I notice a hairbrush in his hand. He hands it to me.

"Thin walls. Jaycee said to bring this to you," he explains and my eyes hone in on his bicep, getting lost in his beauty again. That is until Nick walks over, grabs the brush and with a quick, "Thanks," closes the door in his face.

"Nick! That was rude." I scold and hear Blue's laughter as he goes back to the other room.

"Come here, Abigail," he orders, his voice serious.

His bossiness pisses me off and turns me on at the same time. I get on my tiptoes, right in his face. "What, Nick?"

"Fire," he begins and smiles but then his face gets serious again. "If I catch you checking out another guy again, I will spank your ass," he tells me and I drop back down to my feet and shiver.

"Promise?" I say as I crawl into bed.

"Promise," Nick repeats. "Glad to have my fire back," he whispers against my temple.

CHAPTER THIRTY-ONE

The next morning, Nick tells me he's going to run down to the cabin and grab us some clothes and he'll be back shortly. He gives me a kiss before he leaves and I head for the bathroom. I take a quick three-minute shower starting with washing and conditioning my hair and trying to work out some of the tangles from the bird nest I had last night. I'm feeling so much better. It's almost like those hours on the ledge didn't happen. My back is still a little sore from when I landed, and my face has a slight pink glow from the wind. Otherwise, I'm feeling really good and haven't had to take any pain medication. I know a lot of it has to do with my family being here, Vargas being caught, and of course knowing Nick and I are okay. I smile when step out of the shower and see the toothbrush lying on the counter. I gently pat my skin dry while thinking about spending the day with my family but I wish my grandma and brothers were here. I miss my uncles and aunts and Callie as well, even Blue's family. Sadness begins to take over as I grab Jaycees hairbrush and start brushing my hair.

Nick reenters the room, laughing and carrying some of my clothes with Elvis and Buford on his heels. They come to me and I give them their much deserved head rub while smiling at Nick.

"What's so funny?" I ask, taking my clothes from him.

"Our dads passed out in his study last night and our moms and Lina never made it off the couches after many bottles of wine. They all got drunk. Now, Lina and my mom are at the kitchen table moaning. Your mom was trying to get some coffee started but she keeps holding her head and asking my mom where things are. My mom just kept groaning and telling her to stop yelling," he says and bursts out laughing again. "I started a pot for them." He chuckles again and goes on. "My mom mumbled something about my dad and asked me to find him. Went into the study and your dad is passed out with an almost empty bottle of Jack tucked in beside him and my dad is leaning back in his chair, mouth hanging open with a half empty bottle of Crown cradled like a baby in his arms. I took pictures." He pulls out his phone.

"Seriously?" I ask.

"Seriously," Nick shows me the pictures and we both start cracking up.

After we get dressed, we head downstairs. Jaycee and Blue are coming out of their room at the same time and my sister and I link arms. Nick and Blue follow behind while Elvis and Buford lead the way.

A familiar voice floats up to meet us. "Y'all are ridiculous. Don't drink if you can't handle it. Drink this." I take off running past the dogs, Nick and Blue hollering out for me to slow down and the dogs barking at me telling me to slow down in doggy language. I run into the kitchen and see her.

"Grandma," I yell out excitedly and everyone in the room cusses. Nick's dad falls out of his chair and my dad leaves the room almost crawling and obviously not knowing what direction to go in because he bumps into several walls and changes directions a few times before vanishing around the corner leading to the walk-in pantry. Everyone shushes me except my grandma. She comes over and pulls me into a hug. I can't help but get emotional, but I hold it together when she gently pats my face and walks back over to the counter where she's lined up a row of small glasses and is dropping Alka Seltzer in them and handing them out to everyone.

"Going to have you take an oil and milk bath, sweetheart. That'll help a lot," she says while calling my dad and Ronan back into the room. They grab their glasses and leave again, mumbling their thanks. China's mom is looking at her glass like it's about to come alive and attack her.

"Too late," she says and gets up and runs out of the room.

Lina grabs her cane and walks towards the stairs. "I can't. I just can't," she says and then falls back against the wall, startled when the front door opens and Red, Huck and Levi enter.

"Babe," Red grins in understanding, picking her up and giving her the cane to hold while he carries her up the stairs where they disappear. *Damn, they're a hot looking couple.*

Star and Darcy enter and take in the scene. "Guess we won't be shopping today." Star observes, disappointed.

"Maybe later, much later," my mom replies as Jaycee help her up. "Let's get you back to bed for a while, hmmm?"

"Yes, that would be good. Very, very good and necessary." They start for the door. "Come back in about a week. I should be good as new by then. And Jaycee check those bottles. I drink wine all the time. I think that was some home grown stuff. My God," she whispers in pain. Jaycee softly laughs.

"You got it. I'll go out back and check for a moonshine still and I'll report back in a week," she teases.

"Good, good. Let me know," my mom says dead serious.

"Going to let the dogs out and then I'll get your dad from the pantry and take him upstairs to lie down with your mom. I'll be back," Nick tells me, chuckling. He lets the dogs out before heading to the pantry with Blue following.

CHAPTER THIRTY-TWO

It's almost dinner time and while mine, Nick and Linc's parents are still sleeping off their hangovers, the girls and I have been hanging out with my grandma in the kitchen while she gets dinner ready and the guys are off doing guy things down at one of the barns.

In normal grandma mode, she's taken charge and insisted on cooking for all of us. We're all in our mid-twenties and up but we're still kids to her. All that adult crap goes out the window when she walks in the door. After looking around the kitchen, Grandma decided on making porcupine balls which had me jumping for joy. I love porcupine balls. She found enough hamburger meat to make two pans, plenty for everyone. She pulled out a huge bag of potatoes and had Star and I peel and boiled them for mashed potatoes while Darcy and Delta cleaned the green beans and started on a salad. Jaycee was assigned to make a couple of pitchers of sweet tea and cut up a few lemons. While I'm rinsing off some of the mixing bowls we used in preparing the mashed potatoes, I get a whiff of something that burns my eyes and nose. Grandma is dumping entire bottles of pepper sauce and Tabasco sauce into the mixture for the porcupine balls.

"Grandma, what are you doing?" I hiss, alarmed. That's not going to go down very well with the non-living upstairs that have been cursing Jack, Jim and the Greeks all day.

"Just eat from the blue pan not the red. Red means hot, blue means cold. Remember that. Kids eat from the blue pan, Abigail. Pass it around to your little friends," she tells me as she squishes together the sauce, meat, rice with her hands and starts rolling them into balls and placing them in the red pan. The blue pan is covered with foil and ready for the oven. *Oh shit.* She's going to punish them for drinking too much. I need to remember that if I ever drink too much and she offers to cook for me.

I stop washing dishes to pass around the warning as she instructed. As I tell them what she did, everyone laughs. When dinner is ready, my grandma has us set the table and call for the men to come back from the barn while she goes upstairs to get the "drunks" as she calls them. *Damn, she's mad at them.* About the time we get the table set and get the food set up on the buffet, the men, come through the back door.

Nick comes to my side and plants a hot kiss on my lips that has me blushing. I ask him how things are down at the barn and he tells me their mare still hasn't given birth and he's starting to worry. If nothing happens in the next twenty-four hours he's calling the vet.

"Boys, wash up," Grandma orders and all the men spread out heading for the kitchen and bathroom sinks to clean up with no complaining. I guess grandma's hold some type of grand power or magic. When the men return, we all make it into the dining room at the same time. Mine and Nick's parents come in with Lina following. *Oh, Lina.* No. I have to warn her. She's too sweet for the red pan. I start to warn her, but my grandma picks up a plate and starts putting food on it. When she gets to the blue pan she scoops up a little and hands it to Lina. *Whew.*

Nick's watching me. He sees my conflict and mouths, "What?" as he looks around. All I can do is shake my head, trying not to let anyone know. "Huh?" he says in a whisper.

"Nothing, Nick," I whisper back. "Shhhh." I hiss and grab a plate.

My dad and Ronan start loading up their plates and I freeze. I gather my senses and look around and see everyone has made their plates and is taking their seats. My eyes flash to the buffet and both pans are more than half empty and my eyes go wide and my mouth drops open. I didn't warn everyone and now I don't know who got what. I quickly look back at Nick but my eyes go to Jaycee as she grabs the pitchers of sweet tea and heads to the table. As she walks by me she says in a high pitched whisper, "Too late," and keeps walking without missing a step.

Nick's staring at me with a frown and his eyes drawn together. "What?" he demands again.

"It's your fault," I say and point at him.

"Of course it is," he says and continues loading up his plate. I watch him, half of me wanting him to take from the red and half of me wanting him to take from the blue. He takes from the blue. I've left it up to fate and fate was on his side. I make my plate and sit down next to Nick at the table. Everyone has waited so we can say grace. When I finally take my seat, we all gather hands and my dad says his traditional before dinner prayer.

"Come Lord Jesus, be our guest and let this food to us be blessed," which is just a step up from, "Rub-a-dub-

dub-thanks for the grub," but I always say an extra few words and I'm sure God doesn't mind as long as we mean it. I pick at my food as I look around the table. Grandma places her napkin neatly in her lap and then takes a sip of her iced tea while watching my dad out of the corner of her eye. When he spears a forkful of the porcupine ball, my eyes go wide and so do my grandma's along with Jaycee, Delta, Darcy and Star's. We all stare as he starts to put it in his mouth, but suddenly sniffs it and makes a face.

"Mom?" he asks.

"Yes, honey?" she answers innocently.

"You do realize that Dad warned us that you'd pour pepper juice or Tabasco sauce into our food if we pissed you off," he tells her, chuckling.

"He did not!" she says, surprised.

"Oh yes. Without a doubt he did."

"Well, darn," she laughs.

"It's okay. We deserved it," my dad admits and leans over and kisses her cheek. "Love you, mom. Thanks for dinner." He takes a bite of the porcupine ball, accepting his punishment and then winks at my grandma which makes her laugh.

"Going in for seconds," Levi says and Huck, Blue and Linc follow.

Violet, Lina and China glance around in question as Red grabs his ice tea and downs it.

"It's good stuff. Got a bite to it," Red comments and forks up some more. Lina scoots over her glass of sweet tea so it can be at the ready for him if he needs it. He winks at her. "Thanks babe," he says.

"You're welcome, honey," she replies as she forks up some beans. A huge smile spreads across Red's face as a secret moment passes between them. *Oh, my God, these two are killing me. They're so in love.*

"Thanks for making dinner, Grandma Lila," Ronan says. "It's spicy, but really good," he says which sets off the entire table to compliment my grandma's cooking and say their thank you's.

While China and Violet get my grandma settled in a guest room upstairs, the rest of us pack up our stuff and head back out. Since my grandma is here and our dads have decided not to drunk sleep in the study and our moms in the living room, rooms are needed. There are six bedrooms in the main house, one being the master so now they can take those. Jaycee and Blue are going to spend their last night at our cabin and Delta and Linc are heading back to his place while Star and Huck, and Darcy and Levi head down to the cabins. They thought it would be cool to sit around the campfire but Nick put a halt to that idea saying there was no way I was going to be outside in the cold which they all agreed was best. I haven't done it in a while, and I'm a bit disappointed in myself, so tonight I'm hitting my knees and thanking God for allowing me to be here, and that I came away almost unscaved after hours on that ledge. God was protecting me. As we walk outside and start loading up our cars with our bags, Red helps Lina into his truck and then tosses her bag in the bed. They don't head towards the front gate that leads off the property, but instead to his place down the road. *Killing me, those two are.* I shake my head and smile as I get in the truck. The weather is in the high sixties today and there's no wind. Crazy that three nights ago a blizzard hit and then two nights ago I almost died from the cold. Texas...

CHAPTER THIRTY-THREE

The girls and I decide to go into town tomorrow to do some Christmas shopping. When talking over lunch we realized none of had done any shopping at all. My grandma, Jaycee and my mom and dad are heading out the day after tomorrow but there's talk of them coming back for Christmas or us all going to San Antonio. Nash has been on-duty but called me last night and told me he'd come up and visit as soon as he got some time off. Dad said Chase and Bradley stayed behind to run the shop, McGinty Construction, while he's gone. A few things are going on with Jaycee and Blue's house that they needed to stay and oversee but Bradley and Connor are finally on their honeymoon, planning on a visit at Christmas too when Connor can finally take some time off from the hospital. Like usual, Jake and Jesse are off somewhere saving the world. *God, I really miss them all.*

Later that night, Nick pulls some steaks from the freezer and heads out to the deck with Blue to grill them.

Jaycee and I stay inside; Nick doesn't want me in the cold even a little. We wrap up some potatoes in foil and pop them in the oven on blast so they'll be done in time to eat with the steaks. Searching for something else to make with dinner, I spot a few Bud Lights in back of the fridge; I grab four and hand two to Jaycee. We both grab our coats and head out to the deck even if only for a few moments. Most of the snow has melted from the deck and Blue is leaning against the rail watching Nick work at the grill. Jaycee hands Blue his beer and I hand Nick his.

"Thanks darlin', but don't want you out here long, okay?" he instructs and pops the top and takes a pull.

"You're welcome and I know," I say and snuggle into him and glance at Jaycee. She has a shining glow on her face as she looks over the railing. *What the hell?* I separate from Nick and walk over next to Jaycee, peer over the rail and then squeal. "You have a pool, Nick? You didn't tell me you had a pool." There's steam rising up from the water and I can barely contain my excitement. "And it's heated? We've got to go swimming. Did you bring your suit?" I ask Jaycee and she looks at me like I'm crazy. "Okay. Yeah. I have a couple. You can borrow one." I start for the house but I'm grabbed from behind.

"How about we go swimming tomorrow? I just turned the heater on. It'll need to warm overnight, darlin'. Not taking a chance at you getting sick after everything," Nick kisses me on my head before turning back to the grill. "These are ready. Let's eat." I take the plate of steaks from Nick and he grabs our beers and we all head inside. I grab the potatoes and Nick gets another round of beers before we take our seats. This is our first dinner together in 'our' home. The first meal we cooked together. Our first dinner guests. So many firsts. Nick is starting at me probably sharing the same thoughts.

Later that night, I hit my knees again and thank God for all his amazing blessings and for keeping me safe on that ledge. Dr. Santos explained falling down into that ridge and landing on that little ledge probably saved my life as I was hidden from the freezing winds. I know that God, He had me the entire time. Faith, I should have more.

CHAPTER THIRTY-FOUR

The next day, all the girls head into town but I'm waiting on Nick. He left before I woke to check on something down at the barn. He wants to see before I leave and said he'd bring his Jeep back for me to use. His perfectly fine truck is sitting out front but he doesn't want me driving it saying it's not safe for me because it has quirks I don't know yet. Jaycee calls me and says all the girls are meeting at Zink's for lunch and to not worry. Just meet them there and we'd go back to the mall together. China suggested I go up to the main house and grab her little rental car. She rode in with Lina and my mom so it's just sitting there. I text Nick and tell him I'm going to drive his truck just up to the main house and grab his mom's rental car and then head into town. When he gets my text, he calls me and apologizes for taking so long and tells me to go for it and then proceeds to give me twenty minutes' worth of instructions on how to drive his truck the one mile to his parents:

- Tap the dash three times before you turn the key.
- as you turn the key, pump the gas pedal twice, only twice, otherwise you'll flood her and she'll wait another hour to start
- half pump the break before actually pumping the brake when you go to stop otherwise...
- when you get where you need, rub the steering wheel and thank her ;)

I laugh at the last instruction, even though I can tell he's serious. Oh, my Lord. I grab my coat, purse and the keys and head out to the truck. I get in and a strange feeling comes over me so rather than test "her" thinking Nick is being ridiculous, I tap the dash three times before I turn the key. When she starts right up I put her in gear and start up to the road. I'm halfway when I see an armadillo leisurely crossing and I let off the gas, slowing down.

The armadillo watches me and the closer I get, it decides to stop and stand unmoving in the middle of the road. This armadillo has a death wish or it's challenging me to a game of chicken. I push on the brakes forgetting to half pump it first and the truck keeps going. As I get closer to the armadillo it still doesn't move so I swerve into the dirt and around the armadillo while still pushing on the brake

251

but not stopping for another few yards. *Oh shit!* When I finally get her to stop, I sit back in the seat and allow the feelings in my legs to come back before I turn her off.

"No hard feelings, okay?" I grab my stuff and get out of truck to walk the rest of the way up the road. The 'asshole the armadillo' is gone, nowhere to be seen. *Okay?*

Me: *Your truck is sitting halfway between our cabin and your parents. Talk to you later. Love you.* I text Nick and smile when his response is immediate.

Nick: *What happened?*

Me: *Oh, I hit the brakes to avoid killing an armadillo taking ten years to cross the road. Took your truck about the same amount of time to stop.*

Nick: *Yeah, that armadillo is a dick. It's always pulling that shit. But you're okay?*

Me: *What??? I'm fine grabbing you mom's rental and heading into town with the girls.*

Nick: *Okay. Have fun. Love you. xo*

I smile at his xo and with a sappy grin I quickly type back.

Me: *Love you too xoxoxoxoxox*

I tuck my phone in my pocket and walk into the mudroom and look on the key rack for the rental keys. Spotting the rental companies tag, I take them and walk out front to the red Dodge Dart sitting in the driveway. I hop in and not long after turning off the drive onto the road, dinging sounds from the dash. The fuel light is blinking and with a sigh, I pull into the first gas station I see. I roll up to the pump and look for the lever to open the tank but can't find it. Getting out, I notice I've parked on the wrong side so I hop back in and turn the car around. Once I get it lined up next to the pump I take another quick look for lever but still don't see one. There's no lip on the gas cap to open, leaving me perplexed. I can't find anything. Trunk, yes. Hood, yes. Gas cap, no. *What the shit?* My phone goes off and I see it's a text from Jaycee.

Jaycee: *Where are you?*

Me: *Getting gas. Be there soon*

I toss my phone down on the seat next to me. I can't be bothered now. I'm on a mission. I continue looking for a button, lever, and thinking voice command I call out, "Open gas cap. Gas cap open," like an idiot to the car and of course nothing happens. Maybe it's touch screen. I touch everything even if it's not a screen, but I stop myself from

253

touching the windows, there's no way. I release the hood, open the sunroof, set the childproof locks, pop open the trunk, reset all the radio stations and wash the widows and when nothing works I start messing with the ac and cruise controls and look back at the widows—no—maybe. What am I missing?

Vehicles are coming and going all around me. They're getting their gas, a drink, probably grabbing some jerky, living an entire lifetime and me, still here, staring at the steering wheel pushing on what I know are screws and bolts, but still I try. I get back out of the car and stomp over to the gas cap and run my fingers along the seam. Nope, no secret lip has appeared. As I stand there I think, manual. The car has a manual. I sit in the passenger's seat, laughing like a mad woman. *I've got you now Dodge Dart!* But as I go through the manual, I find nothing about the gas cap. I check the index, nope. Everything but the gas cap. This makes no sense. *What the fuck?* I turn the manual over, conceding to the fact that I'm going to have to call someone. I decide to see if there's 1-800 number rather than calling Nick and embarrassing myself. He'd never let me live this down. I find the number for customer service but decide to try one more time. *God, I feel like an idiot.* I stand in front of the gas cap, hands on my hips willing the answer to come to me when an arm comes up over my shoulder and the hand attached to that arm pushes in on the gas cap with one finger, one damn finger, and it pops open.

What. The. Fuck Is. This? Are you kidding? I hang my head in shame. I'd like to complain and say I almost had it, but that would be a lie. I was nowhere near to trying that. I turn around with a thankful smile on my face. I jump and scream when I see the person attached to the hand and who he's with, not even caring when chuckles break out all around us.

"Jake! Jesse! What are you doing here?" I squeal.

CHAPTER THIRTY-FIVE

Jake wraps me up in a hug and I start crying. God, I've missed him. "Hey, now. It's okay," Jake soothes me.

"I've missed you so much is all," I tell him before embracing Jesse.

"Hey, runt," he greets me and kisses my head. No sooner does he put me down and wipe my tears then the sound of motorcycles fills the air as they pull into the gas station and surround us. *Oh, my God!* As Chase and Nash turn off and dismount their bikes, I run over and slam into Nash right as he gets both feet on the ground. The men in our family are close but Chase and I, we have a bond all our own since we were the only two living with my mom and dad. He pulls me into a hug and just holds me while I cry.

"I missed you. I haven't seen you in forever," I say to Chase.

"You've been here less than a week, Abigail." He laughs but pulls me closer.

"No! It's been much longer than that!" I complain. "No, it's hasn't. I know." I concede and let him go while wiping my face and laughing. Johnny and Acer are observing the scene with matching grins. "Hey, y'all." Embarrassed stains my cheeks but I brush it off. "What are y'all doing here?" I ask Jake and Jesse.

"Dad called Nash, said you ran off, but then called back and said you slid off...the side of a ridge. Really, Abigail and got yourself trapped? Nash tracked us down and told us what was going on. I was due back in a week and Jesse in a couple of days but we each talked to our commanding officers' and they released us early. We're both on leave till after Christmas. Wanted to see you, spend a couple of days here and then head back home and see a couple of people before heading back out." he explains.

"A couple?" Jesse laughs.

"More like one person. A very pretty person?" Nash says and Jake blushes. Yes, my badass soldier brother blushed.

"What? Wait! Who?" I ask looking between all of them.

"Her name is Kore," Chase adds. "And she's not pretty, she's beautiful."

257

"Well, how did y'all meet? How serious is it? Can we meet her?" I ask causing my brothers to laugh and Jake to put up his hands to slow me down.

"Of course you can meet her, but I just got back and I wanted to see my baby sisters' first is that okay?" he half jokes.

"No, Jake that's not okay. Call her. Ask her up," I demand. "Jake, Jaycee and I have been waiting for this moment. We have a test and she has to pass it, or else," I say in seriousness but wink at him when he looks worried. "I'm actually serious though. Jaycee and I will test her, but we'll just make one up. We don't have it on paper or anything. We'll wing it," I point at him. "Call her. I want to meet her," I slap him on the chest before turning and grabbing the gas nozzle. Before pumping the gas, I reach for my debit card from my purse. Jesse beats me and swipes his instead. "Thanks," I tell him and smile. He gives me one of his famous smirks that say, *that's right, I'm the man*, causing me to roll my eyes. Deciding I have to or I won't sleep tonight; I close the gas cap and then push it open with my finger. Yep, that's all it took. I shake my head at myself before I start pumping the gas. "Plus, Jaycee and Grandma will want to meet her, too," I call out over my shoulder.

"Well, here's the thing. I've already asked her up and you've kind of already met her," Jake informs me. "I'm kind of worried of how Jaycee is going to react. I need to talk to her."

"Why, Jake? Jaycee would want nothing more for you to be happy and in love," I remind him, while still pumping the gas. He looks into my eyes and I can see he's genuinely worried. "Who is it?" I ask, now getting worried myself. I put the nozzle back and close the gap before giving him my undivided attention.

"Kore was one of Jaycee nurses when she was in the hospital recovering. Corporal Blass," he says and my heart skips a beat. Of course. I get it now. He's worried it's going to bring back memories or flashbacks and upset Jaycee. He's so sweet. Our Jake.

"Jake, never would Jaycee ever want you to hold back from any type of love or happiness. I think we all underestimate Jaycee," I reassure him. "I say, talk to her. Not for her, but for you. I know her. She'll welcome Kore with open arms. I've only seen you with a couple of women and they weren't around long enough for me to even find out their name so if Kore really means something to you, talk to Jaycee."

"Yup," Acer chimes in. "Girl's smart."

"Alright, so where are y'all going because I'm heading to the mall to go shopping. Want to come with me?" I ask. They all grunt and head back to their rides. "Already talked to Blue. Meeting him at the ranch. Nick's going to show us around and then we're all meeting up at a diner called *Zink's* for dinner at seven o'clock. He said we'd come into town and eat since you'd all be busy shopping. I dropped Ana off and she's with Jaycee now," Acer says.

"We were driving by and saw you at the pump so we pulled in across the street and watched. It was pretty entertaining. Wanted to see what you would actually do when you still couldn't get it open but Jake had enough and him and Jesse drove over." Johnny tells me.

"Yeah, would have been here all night. Wasn't even warm," I joke but I'm totally serious. "Well I'll see you later then," I call out as I get in the car with a huge smile on my face and my heart and stomach fluttering in happiness. I just wish the others were here too. Next weekend I'm going to try and convince Nick into driving down to San Antonio. That way we can get my car too. Happy with my plan, I head to the mall and meet up with the ladies. I do some serious damage to my bank accounts but get a lot done. Life is good.

CHAPTER THIRTY-SIX

Most everyone is inside *Zink's* chatting away at the five tables Bubbles connected so our families could sit together. Nick isn't here yet but he's on his way. He's been in the barn all day tending to the mare that's due any moment. From what he's told me, and what I know from school, she's right at the point of causing distress to the foal if she doesn't give birth. Nick called a neighbor and ranch hand, Dawson to watch over the mare while he comes into town for dinner.   He spoke to the vet earlier and as soon as he gets back into town from escorting a client to a cattle auction in Abilene, he'll be over to check on her. The beam of headlights alerts me to Nick's arrival. I start towards the parking lot to meet him but stop when I see he's not alone. It's too dark to see a face and everyone is inside so I have no clue that is with him until he opens his door and a high pitched squeal of joy fills the air.

"Aunt Abby! It's me. Knuckle Nick, Hurwe." Callie squeals.

"Hang on, princess. These dam-rn straps. Oh, thank God," Nick says and then sets a wiggling Callie on the ground.

She looks between him and me, her eyes huge, waiting, while skip jumping. "Hurwe, I can't go by myself." She pulls Nick's hand from the Jeep as my uncle Brock steps out of the passenger side and pulls the lever and out pops my beautiful aunt Paige.

My hands go to my mouth because I'm about to squeal like Callie, then deciding what the hell. "Princess Callie, come here!" Nick points at me, giving her the okay and she takes off running full speed towards me. I kneel down just in time for her to launch herself into my arms. We hug for a moment and then I stand with her still wrapped around me.

"Look!" she says and holds out her leg, "Mommy got us matching Uff boots." She points to her boots. Oh, my God, too cute, is all I can think when I look down. Both of them have on tan and leopard print Ugg boots with bows on the back and fur along the top. Callie, as always, is dressed adorable. My aunt has her in blue jeans tucked into her Uggs, and her coat and mittens are both tan and her coat has a leopard print collar. To top it off, her beautiful blonde hair is hanging all the way down her back and she's wearing a wide leopard headband holding the front of her hair back. Her tiny ears are covered in tan furry ear muffs.

"In my defense, doesn't she look adorable?" Aunt Paige asks.

"She's more than adorable. We need to make up a new word for what she is," I say and tickle Callie until she starts laughing and wiggling. She swings around and puts her hands out for Nick to take her. "Guess she's had enough of me," I say and laugh as I hand her back.

"Taking her in. Don't be long," he says as he looks over at my uncle Brock who hasn't moved.

Aunt Paige walks with Nick who has Callie hitched on his hip into *Zink's*. When they clear the door, Callie squeals again. "Knuckle Max!" She squirms out of Nick's arms and runs to Blue who picks her up and starts smothering her with kisses.

My heart and body fill with the love for my family. I'd missed them this last week when everything bad happened. It's like I got depleted of the McGinty support and togetherness and now I feel myself filling back up. Uncle Brock looks relieved; he's been standing there with his hands tucked in his front pocket, watching me. He opens his arms and I accept his embrace happily. Where Uncle Duke and Jaycee have their connection, Uncle Brock and I have ours. We're the babies of the family. We've been spoiled and sheltered all our lives. Sometimes I think too much. We were never given the opportunity to spread our wings. Both of us are much stronger than the others think. More than we thought. Uncle Brock never broke when he and Aunt Paige couldn't conceive and they lost their babies. When precious Cole passed away Uncle Brock stood next to that angel and made him his son. He stayed strong and moved forward and never gave up dreaming of being a parent. He called agencies, churches, checked all avenues to make sure he and Aunt Paige had a family and I know if Callie wouldn't have come along, they'd still be fine. He'd make sure of it. He didn't know, but I was watching him and the entire time, he never blinked. He might be considered the college boy to the family, but he's my model.

"You okay?" he asks as he pulls me out of our embrace.

"I am. I really am," I say and smile.

"Good," he replies, pinching my chin. "Let eat. Nick couldn't say enough about the chicken fried steak and I'm starving," he drapes his arm around me as we walk to the door. 'I'm proud of you, Abigail." he whispers right before we go in.

"I watched you, Uncle Brock. You taught me. Thank you and I'm proud of you too," I say and lean into him.

His body tenses and then he lets out a deep breath. "Thank you," he whispers and we walk in and join the others.

CHAPTER THIRTY-SEVEN

Halfway through dinner, Callie starts yawning. It's her normal bedtime but throw in being passed around the table and chatting up a storm with everyone and she's yawning more than usual.

Of course when she saw Levi and Huck she had to introduce herself. She's sitting in Huck's lap eating his corn on the cob while wearing Levi's hat. But most of her time has been with Linc, her brother. Lina, being the sweet, wonderful woman she is has done nothing but love and enjoy her like all of us, even knowing that she was conceived while her husband was having an affair with another woman.

I can already see Delta falling in love with her too. Knowing this beautiful little girl will be the aunt to her and Linc's baby. Linc and Uncle Brock stand up from the table and walk to the side of the diner to talk privately. When they're finished, Linc approaches Aunt Paige and whispers something in her ear. She nods but she adds a smile and then he looks at Blue and Jaycee.

Linc calls Callie over to him and he squats down to her level. I don't know what he's saying but the smile on her face tells me she's happy about it. I watch her, like everyone else, smiling at her joy. The cowbell on the door clanks and I turn to see who it is, my smile falling. I'm not sure how I'm supposed to react when I see Santino Vargas walk into the diner followed by Daniel "Rocky" Jennings. Rocky stops and looks around, scanning the diner.

"Bwother," Callie calls out and his eyes find hers. His face lights up and he undergoes a transformation. He's no longer the scary man covered in tattoos with long hair and a beard that we all know did bad things. No, in this moment, when he picks up Callie and she grabs his face and kisses him smack on the lips, which makes him chuckle, I finally see him, I see Daniel. Not Rocky and not Shadow. He looks years younger as he listens to her, her hands telling a story and unlike some adults who only pretend to listen, he's listening like his life depends on it. Like her little voice is the most beautiful thing in the world. I laugh when she sticks out her leg and shows him her boots and then point at my aunt Paige. She's been watching and smiling and when Callie points to her she sticks her leg out so Rocky, or now Daniel, can see her boots too.

He's not looking at the boots when he nods and mouths a thank you to her. She smiles and begins talking to Violet and my grandma while Daniel takes Callie over to a booth and sits her down on the table in front of him. He pulls off his coat and relaxes as Callie goes on and on.

Bubbles walks over with a sweet tea and sets it on the table but his eyes, a beautiful silver with stars, just like Callie's, never leave hers as he says thank you. He just stares at Callie with a beautiful smile as she babbles on about nothing. She takes a rare breath and looks down at his arm and her face turns curious. She points to a tattoo and traces the letters with her fingers. From where I'm sitting I can see it clearly, it says Callie in beautiful script with a beautiful intricate knot that is Celtic. I've seen it before because Jaycee and I researched getting matching tattoos and that was one we liked. It means 'sister'.

Callie sees another one and pushes up his sleeve. I feel my heart get heavy when I see it. It's the Celtic symbol for brother only he's added blue angel wings to it and underneath in the same beautiful script, Cole. Nick catches my and we both take a breath. Deep.

Finally, Callie breaks out into a yawn and falls forward on Daniel's shoulder. She snuggles into his neck and yawns again. He lets her lay like that for a few minutes but then pulls her back and says something to her. A sleepy, goofy grin crosses her face as she nods. He holds her tired little body with one arm as he pulls the box Jaycee gave to Linc last night out of his pocket and opens it. He removes a silver necklace with a cross pendant with an emerald in the center. He undoes the clasp and I notice the entire diner has gone dead quiet. Everyone is watching and most of the women are crying. Daniel wraps it around her little neck, fastens the clasp and then fixes her hair around the chain.

His eyes glassy are as she picks up the pendant and stares it for a couple moments before falling back into his chest. Callie is the 'special girl' his mamo told him that he should one day give it to. He sits back against the booth and looks out the diner window as he rubs her back until she's sound asleep. When he goes to stand, everyone begins talking softly. Daniel walks over to my uncle Brock and hands Callie to him, but not before giving her a kiss on her head. Moving to his mom's side, he kisses her cheek and then takes a final look around the room and without saying a word, walks out the door. Santino, who had been talking to Delta gives everyone a wave and then follows him out. We all sit quiet looking at the door as the sound of motorcycles start and still no one says anything as they fade off into the distance.

"Take care of him God," I whisper my prayer up to Heaven.

CHAPTER THIRTY-EIGHT

After the heavy emotion at dinner, we all decide to go to a bar up the street for a few drinks to relax. Well everyone except the "drunks". My grandma made them all go with her which they said was fine because they're tired. Tired meaning still not ready to take the road to hangover'ville again. So when all the "grownups" and a sleeping Callie load in the cars and head back at the ranch, the rest of us leave our cars and walk to *DJ's Saloon*. It's a cool old style saloon just like the movies. The entire place is wood and it even has a second floor but not for "paying customers" but for the restrooms and office. We pull a few tables together and sit down. A very pretty waitress complete with feathers in her hair, sexy dress cut all the way up the front so she's flashing her fishnet covered legs and a garter comes over to take our order and I decide either I need to work here, or Nick needs to let me buy that outfit and wear it around the house whenever I'd like. I love it and she's hot. I want to be hot like her. When she comes to me for my order, I say "I'd like a Bud Light and a job application." She giggles at my request. When she smiles, she has the loveliest dimples that compliment her green eyes.

"Job application?" she asks.

"I love your outfit. I want one. If I have to work here to get one, I will." I tell her.

"No. You won't." Nick says from beside me.

"Um, excuse me?" I say to Nick.

"No way in hell are you working here," he declares.

"Why not?" I ask but can't help but giggle at the look on his face. It's like he's ready to have a breakdown dealing with me.

"You've just earned a spanking, fire," he warns.

"Okay, honeysuckle," I lean in and kiss him. "I just wanted the outfit. Calm down," I say and turn back to the waitress.

Nick mumbles. "Still spanking your ass tonight."

"Okay. I guess I deserve it," I wink at the waitress. She cracks up as she walks away.

It's getting later and we've all had a couple of rounds and are joking around and laughing having a good time. Well, not Delta. She's seconds away from reaching over and strangling Darcy. Darcy has been taunting her all night. She's been talking about how good her margarita is and apparently that's Delta's favorite. Every time Linc looks over at Delta and sees her pouting he starts laughing which isn't helping the situation. Things don't get much better when Star adds in that she can have one and then inserts a dramatic pause before saying...in seven and half more months.

"I'll be right back. Going to have the bartender make her a virgin margarita. It might help a little and also save Darcy's life." Jaycee jokes before heading off to the bar.

Levi and Huck get up and head upstairs to the bathroom and Nick hollers after them. "Thought only the girls went to the restroom in pairs." Levi turns around and flips Nick the bird but is laughing along with Huck when he does it. "Yeah, go talk through those anger emotions out and then fix your lips before you come back down," he calls out again and everyone cracks up.

I'm leaning into Nick and we're talking to Blue and Johnny while Jaycee is still at the bar getting Delta her non-alcoholic margarita when a group of women start towards our table with a fake bleach blonde leading the way. Nick tenses and grabs hold of me like he's scared of them. It only takes a moment for me to realize this must be Ashley and her brood of bitches. That whining Tina from Wal-Mart is with them. Delta's face is turning red as Darcy and Star hold her down. I'm more than ready to meet this bitch. I don't react, just keep my relaxed pose against Nick while rubbing his thigh, wanting him to stay calm and not react, too. I got this, honeysuckle.

Ashley looks around the table and then at Nick before her eyes come to mine. I raise my eyebrow and tilt my head in warning but she doesn't notice it or doesn't heed it. I wait and think back at how I lashed out at Nick because of her. I have a quick, Irish temper and he suffered from her lies. That realization only pisses me off more.

"So, I'm—" Ashley begins.

"A bitch," I say and nod before going on. "Yes, we all know. Thanks for stopping by."

Soft laughter and giggles can be heard around the table but I keep my eyes on Ashley. Her mouth drops open before she narrows her eyes on me. I watch and wait and then she starts again.

"You should know Delta and N—" she tries again.

"I know," is all I say.

"You don't know," she argues.

"But I do, Ashley. I know you're pathetic and repulsive. I can understand why, when you thought you had a shot, which was completely delusional, you took it. He told me what you tried and you know what happened when he did?" I wait and when she says nothing I go on, "We spent the entire night making love."

My brothers groan and I hear mutterings of *no, that's wrong, just fucking wrong and fuck* from all of them, but I ignore them. "Never thought of you once. You're a joke and a loser. Please, go away now," I dismiss her.

"Listen here, you stupid bitch, I—" is all Ashley gets out before she's laying on the ground and Darcy is holding her hand.

"Oh, my God, that hurt. I didn't know it was going to hurt," Darcy whines.

Levi takes her hand. "Babe, how many margaritas have you had?" he asks while his body shakes with laughter.

"One," she tells him.

"One? I don't think so, honey," he says smiling at her.

"One for me and two and a half for Delta," she says then breaks down in a drunken laugh.

"Hey, what the hell? You can't hit Ashley," Tina complains as she leans down and helps Ashley up.

"Yeah, who the hell do you think you are coming in here thinking you can replace us? We'll mop up—" the very short girl with red hair says while jabbing her finger at me but stops and grabs her cheek when Jaycee full on bitch slaps her.

"Don't you point your finger at my sister like that, you ugly leprechaun," she warns. She jumps around, blowing on her hand. "What the hell? You guys make it look so easy." Blue positions his body between the girls and Jaycee giving her his protection. He's grinning while checking her hand.

"Love, that's only in the movies." he says chuckling when she frowns at him.

"Well why didn't you tell me before I did it?" she demands.

"Didn't know you were going to do it, Love. And leprechaun? We need to maybe work on your insults. You're not in kindergarten. You're an adult now," he says and kisses her palm.

Ashley walks over to a table full of guys and points to us while saying something and holding her cheek. They guys all look at her, then us before rising from their chairs and heading over to us with the most unfriendly looks; the biggest guy of them leading the way. *Oh, no.* Chairs scrape behind me as all the guys at our table stand up. Levi and Huck choose the right moment to rejoin us.

Linc pulls Delta over to the bar and tells her to stay put. She puts her hands on her hips and glares at him. "Seriously I'm a trained special agent with the FBI!" she reminds him and starts back towards us.

Linc stops her. "No, doll, you're the beautiful mother of my unborn child. Please stay here and stay safe," he requests softly.

Delta's face turns from angry to sweet as she leans in and kisses Linc. A beautiful moment but short lived when Ashley interrupts. "That's not Linc's baby, you slut, that's Nick's!" she spits her lie and I've had enough.

My Irish temper kicks in and I punch Ashley in the face and then grab her hair and start yanking. The guys from the other table start towards us but Blue, Johnny, Jake and Jesse step in front of all of us and face off with them while Nick grabs me.

"Calm down, fire. Let her go." I do as he says and shove her to the ground and turn to help my brothers, I don't want them to get hurt. Jake puts his hands up, as in true Jake form, he's going to try and calm the situation and talk everyone down.

"One chance to walk away. It's all you're going to get. Take it," his voice is soft but his words and tone hold warning.

Yeah, take it boy-bitches or you're going to be crying to your mommas, I think, not say of course. The other men don't listen, just wait as a couple more guys join them causing Linc, Huck, Levi, Nash, Chase and Nick to flank, Jesse, Jake, Blue and Johnny. Damn it's nine against at least twelve.

"I really hate fighting," Jake says and Jesse, Nash and Chase start laughing. "Last chance." Jake says.

The big guy who's just a little smaller than Jake, leans in. "Didn't ask for a chance."

279

"Nope. They sure didn't, Jake," Jesse says.

I watch as Jake nods, and then his arms and legs are flying. Jesse, Johnny and Blue take a step back as Jake takes down the first three without breaking a sweat. When our hot waitress starts over to break up the fight, Jesse steps in and grabs her around the waist and sits back down in his chair with her. At first she starts to fight him but when she gets a look at him, she stops and smiles. He smiles back and then quickly stands back up, sets her down and steps back into the mix and clothes lining a guy who's rushing Jake from behind, then calmly walks back over to our waitress. She's looking at him in awe and he winks at her which causes me to roll my eyes and gag. Jaycee's eyes, like mine, are trained on Jake. He's taken down all but two all by himself and now they're rethinking their involvement and backing away. Nash and Chase are at the bar ordering another beer while Blue and Linc are sitting back down. Levi and Huck are walking off towards the pool table while Delta, Darcy and Star are huddled next to each other watching Jake take down all the guys by himself and licking their lips while Johnny keeps watch over them. Ew, gross, again. About the time the last guy gives up, the Sheriff and two deputies come in the front door. The Sheriff looks around and sees a few of the guys Jake took down dragging themselves from the floor.

The Sheriff, an older man with long gray hair pulled back in a ponytail and tucked underneath a cowboy hat takes another step forward and lets out an irritated huff. He has a salt and pepper goatee and is wearing jeans, cowboy boots and a western shirt with his badge and gun hanging from his belt. He looks down at the men on the floor and then around the room. The two deputies, also in jeans but wearing black polo with the Sheriff's department emblem and badges and guns hanging from their belts, stand back by the door not saying anything.

"What happened?" he asks the guys that have just got up from the floor.

"Nothing. Fell down," the big guy says.

"Fell down," the sheriff says and it's not a question. "All of you. Same exact time. Just fell down."

"Yes, Sheriff," a few of the men say.

"No they didn't!" Ashley screams. "Him!" she screams and points to Jake. "He did it."

"Shut up, Ashley!" one of the other guys shouts.

I'm guessing they don't want anyone else to know all of them were taken down by one guy, but Ashley whines on.

"No. He hurt y'all. Look, you're all bleeding," she says. "You probably need an ambulance. Just stay still in case you have internal bleeding or something and need surgery," she says in a panic. "Someone call 911."

"Ashley, who the hell do I look like?" the Sheriff asks. "I am 911," he says and then mumbles. "Jesus Christ. Elevator doesn't travel to the top on that one."

"Sheriff, arrest him," Ashley says and points at Jake again.

"For what?" he asks while taking a seat in one of the chairs. "Because these boys are clumsy?"
"What? No—" she starts but when of the other a guy's finally barks her name she stops and lets out a huff. "Fine, arrest her, her and her," Ashley says and points to Jaycee, Darcy and me.

"For what? They responsible for you being a nasty little number always causing trouble in the town?" the Sheriff asks.

"No Sheriff, they attacked us," she says and stomps her foot.

"I'll need witnesses and statements otherwise I'm looking at a she said/she said situation. Who saw what?" he asks and pulls a tiny notebook from his shirt pocket and flips open the top. One of the deputy's steps forward and pulls a pen from his pocket and hands it to him.

"Everyone saw it. Take your pick," she says and gestures around the bar. When she does, everyone turns away and goes back to what they're doing.

The Sheriff hands the pen back at the deputy and flips his tiny notebook closed and tucks it back in his pocket before standing. "We good here?" he asks as he looks over at all of us.

A round of yes, yes sirs, yep, and then a boom of hooah's shake the room.

The Sheriff tips his hat and walks back out the door with Ashley and her pack of bitches following.

"Sorry about all that. Damn, that was impressive. You driving? Because I want to buy you a beer," the leader of the others says to Jake and everyone begins shaking hands and laughing. Jake and all guys start talking and

283

wouldn't you know, all military, vets and some active, talking about serving in the military. They head to the bar and stand around while sharing stories.

While that's all happening I find Jaycee and yank her to me. "Did you see that, sissy?" I ask in disbelief.

"What the hell? He's like so sweet and quiet," Jaycee whispers.

"I don't know. I'm slightly alarmed but more impressed," I say and Jaycee nods. We head back over to the bar and grab us another round before heading back to the ranch.

CHAPTER THIRTY-NINE

We all leave DJ's at the same time, the guys shaking hands and agreeing to get together next time everyone's in town and get a softball game going. The girls and I are all huddled together laughing but I stop when I see someone coming up the walk towards us. It's Kore. Her eyes scan our group. Jake breaks through and walks over to her and pulls her in for a kiss and hug which actually make me feel a little gross so I look away.

"Hey everyone, for those who don't know, this is Kore," Jake introduces her.

This is the first time I've seen Kore out of her scrubs and with her hair down. I see it's not a dark brown like it appeared when she wore it up, but a light brown and it's long, like really long and full. It's hanging in waves down her back and shoulder with a slight flip on the tips and she's wearing makeup which I've never seen before. *Holy moly.* She is beautiful. I mean, I knew she was pretty but my Lord.

Her blue eyes are popping under her full lashes and her lips are covered in a shining light pink gloss. She's wearing tight dark jeans tucked into a pair of black and brown two-toned tall leather boots and the fur from boot socks rim the top. A black leather jacket that looks like it was tailored made for her stops just above her waistline showing off her curves and a wide belt with a big silver belt buckle with a rhinestone in the center.

Curious of Jaycee's reaction, I'm please when I see her happy smile. I shake my head in awe of her once again as she's totally unphased by Kore being here. Jaycee steps forward and pulls her into a hug that goes on for a few moments with a silent message being passed between them. When Kore pulls away she smiles at her and waves at Blue who is right behind Jaycee. When she was assigned as Jaycee's nurse in the hospital, we all got to know her, but apparently not as well as Jake. Did not even see them talk once while Jaycee was recovering from Rocky's attack.

"It's good to see you. When did you get here?" I ask her.

"Um, just now. Jake called and told me to head up so I checked flights and saw there was a hop leaving San Antonio for Abilene and I took it. I rented a car from there and drove here. I can turn it in at the rental place here at the airport in the morning. I hope y'all don't mind. I know he's been gone a while since you've seen each other. If y'all want private time to catch up I can go to a hotel and—" A chorus of hell no's stop her from finishing as Jake pulls her close.

"Did you park at *Zink's*? You hungry? Did you eat?" he asks and all his questions have her smiling shyly.

"I'm fine, and I parked at *Zink's* like you told me. I'm parked next to your truck." she says and wraps her arms around him.

"Well then, let's head out. We'll turn your car in before leaving in the morning."

Before leaving the parking lot of *Zink's,* we agree to meet back at the cabins and have a bonfire. Jesse decides to hang back and wait for his new friend, Allison, our waitress who gets off in an hour. Jake and Kore drive her rental and Jesse and Allison are going to drive Jake's truck. I start to worry about Jesse with Allison but my concerns are laid to rest when Darcy, Delta and Star assure me she's been around for awhile and never been anything but nice. I didn't peg her as a serial killer, but you never know. As we start to load in the cars I spot Jaycee talking to Jake. The couple of beers he had tonight must have calmed him enough to talk to her and he probably wants to explain things. He looks worried, but when Jaycee plows into him and wraps her arms around his waist, he smiles and rests his cheek on her head while rubbing her back. I didn't notice at first but she's crying.

I start over, worry filling me but stop when Jaycee speaks. "I'm so happy for you, Jake. You meeting someone and feeling like this, is amazing. This is something good coming from something bad and I'm so happy for that and you. Love you." she says and kisses his cheek. Like I said, Jaycees heart is pure and forgiving and made of steel.

Delta, Nick and Linc decide to drive us all back since they had little or nothing to drink. Jaycee and Blue ride with Nick and I along with Johnny and Chase. I end up on Johnny's lap, since we're all crammed together in the back seat, which doesn't please Nick. His bad mood breaks and he starts laughing along with the others when Jaycee and I start singing, *Take My Drunk Ass Home* by Luke Bryan.

As soon as we pull up to the cabin, Nick is out and pulling me from Johnny's lap. "Really Nick, Blue is like my brother and that's his brother. Calm down, we're practically—" is all I get out before Nick is guiding me away.

"Practically nothing, Abigail. Jesus, now I know how Blue felt and I'm paying for it," he says.

Nick asks Jaycee and me to grab blankets and snacks while he and Blue grab beer and fill up the ice chests. We get everything together and load the Jeep up but Nick has Blue take the Jeep down with Jaycee, Johnny and Chase while he and I go to the barn to check on the mare now I know is named, Shelly. We hitch a ride back up to Nick's truck and as we load inside, Blue is already turning back around and heading back down to the cabins. I scoot in next to Nick for the drive to the barn and see it's lit up so bright it makes the night look like day. We walk in and make our way to Red and two other men standing in front of a stall talking. Nick shakes hands and introduces me to the vet, Dr. Tobin and a very handsome, Dawson. Red steps around us after giving us a quick hello and heads back into Shelly's stall and leans down and rubs her side. Shelly is lying on her side but is restless and keeps looking around. I look over at the vet in concern.

"She's fine, honey. By morning I think. I'll be back around six but if y'all need me, call me. Red said he's staying in the loft so he'll be near her," Dr. Tobin's says and grins before walking out.

"I'm going to stay too; Lanie took the kids and drove down to Wimberley for some shopping or something. Her mom and sister are meeting her there for a ladies' weekend. Happy to pass on that trip," he tells us while leaning down and rubbing Shelly's head.

"Alright then, I'm heading back up but I'll have my phone next to me. Call if anything comes up," Nick says and we start back for the truck after I say bye and take one final look at Shelly.

CHAPTER FORTY

Nick and I park his truck behind his Jeep and hop out and head down where everyone is sitting around the bonfire in chairs and on benches. Someone has lit the chimeneas and pulled out a radio and Randy Houser is singing *How Country Feels* and I laugh at the timing of the song and how fitting it is in this moment. Nick leads me over to an empty chair and pulls me down on his lap while Linc reaches down into a cooler and hands us both a beer. I briefly look up at the beautiful Texas night sky and all of God's beauty before relaxing back into Nick. He wraps his arms around my waist and holds me close while I sit back enjoying all the laughs going on around me. When I start talking to Chase about the secret passages in the main house I gain everyone's attention. Nick tries to tell them the passages were just an architect mistake, but Star isn't having that. She leans forward in her chair and offers to tell everyone the real story. Everyone leans forwards to hear what Star is going to say. Even Nick's arms grow tighter around me and I giggle but at the same time I prepare myself.

The night is quiet and you can't hear a breath coming from anyone as Star tells the story...

"In the 1900's, the south plains were terrorized by dark entities raiding the railroads leaving a trail of death behind them. The sound of the horse's hoofs, almost silent in the night, the only warning terror and death would soon be upon them leaving the passengers innocent to the horror whispering up the train cars towards them. Silent as the wind, they'd board the train and waste no time massacring everyone on board, men, women and even children, saving the conductor for last knowing he had the key to the safe where the passengers' most valuable possessions were kept.

Once he handed over the key, they'd dispose of him too. These soul-less evildoers would toss their victims from the trestle without a thought and blood-curdling screams and cries could be heard throughout the plains as their bodies fell through the dark night only to be silenced when they landed in hushed thumps along the ground below. The townsfolk know the railroad is cursed and haunted by the robber's victims and to this day no one goes near it at night. The victim's souls, they come back. They wait for the sign and then their need for revenge awakens them. Every night, the midnight death train, as we call it, sounds its whistle calling them to rise. If you're very quiet, you can hear the galloping of the horses as they race along the train waiting for their befalling and soon blood-curdling screams follow, not from the undead, but from their victims. It's said, at midnight, if you hear the death whistle, get inside. If you're foolish enough not to heed the legend, be warned. As you look into the night and the breath of a wind blows slight over your skin, you might see a faint shadow galloping on silent hoofs, carrying the devil himself to get you along with his slaves of the night who now ride on his side of dark. But no one has ever stayed out to chance the legend." Star finishes by looking around in warning and then sits back up while Huck has his face buried in her back, laughing.

Smooth as ever Linc asks, "What time is it?"

Johnny pulls out his cell phone. "It's eleven fifty-nine," he whispers.

Nash reaches down for another beer when it happens. A train whistle fills the air and everyone freezes. It sounds a couple more times and I'm laughing but honestly scared shitless as Nick buries himself behind my body in silent laughs. A long horn honk sounds, sending everyone running for the cabins. Even Nick is surprised and picks me up like a sack of potatoes and heads for the cabins while I'm yelling at him to run faster. When laughter hits us we turn and see Jake's truck heading towards us with another car following behind. We're all bent over laughing and catching our breaths when Jesse and Allison get out of their vehicles and walk towards us.

"What's up with y'all?" he asks while smiling in confusion.

"Your timing couldn't have been anymore perfect," Star announces.

"Shit, asshole, why did you honk?" Chase asks clutching his chest.

"An armadillo had his ass parked in the middle of the road and wouldn't move. Sorry?" he says and pulls Allison towards the fire and grabs a beer for them. After a few more nervous laughs, we settle back in. More laughter can be heard as we tell Jesse and Allison what happened and their part in it. Too soon we say our goodbyes for the night but agree to meet at the house around eight for breakfast. I remind to check their food before eating.

Grandma may just be in the mood to give us a lesson this time.

CHAPTER FORTY-ONE

Nick and I along with Jaycee, Blue and Johnny make our way back to our cabin and after giving them a quick tour so they'd know where things were, we settled them into the two guestrooms and make our way to our bedroom. Before I climb into bed, I do as I promised myself I would from now on. I kneel beside the bed and pray. Nick settles next to me and I reach over and take his hands.

"I'm new at this. Not sure what to do," he whispers.

"Me too, but I don't think God has specific rules and guidelines. As long as we're praying, I think He's happy," I whisper back and we hold hands as we send up our silent thank you' to God.

CHAPTER FORTY-TWO

The next morning, we head up to the main house and enjoy breakfast compliments of China, my mom, Grandma and Aunt Paige. Lina and Red are the last ones to arrive as we enjoy the spread of eggs, biscuits and gravy, bacon, sausage and ham, hash browns and grits and of course fruit, yogurt and granola. There's so many of us that we spread out through the dining room, stools at the island with others leaning against the counters holding their plates.

The ones that are finished are doing dishes or relaxing with a mug of coffee.   Kore and Jake are snuggled up against each other and Jesse is quietly talking to a smiling Allison, saying something that has her laughing. I didn't expect to see her here this morning but I found out that they're heading out together. Earlier, Jesse told me he bought a house in Gruene and that shocked me but I'm so glad to know he's settling down. He informed me Allison is moving back home to New Braunfels which is another small town, like Gruene. Those two little towns are literally right next to one another. China must know Allison because I've watched them talk while doing some of the dishes together. Allison looks sad and lost and China pulls her into a hug. The sadness on Allison's face hurts my heart and I glance at Jesse and see he's feeling the same hurt for her. Callie is in Johnny's lap enjoying *his* biscuits and gravy and between bites she wiggles around, anxious for Johnny to give her another bite. Every time he brings the fork to her mouth she opens so wide her eyes go to the ceiling which has him cracking up.

Everyone knows Callie is capable of feeding herself and she does it perfectly well, but that girl, being the princess that she is to all of us, doesn't need to lift a finger especially when all the men are around. China, like me, is now standing back quietly looking around the room with heavy emotion and shiny eyes. I approach her to offer some moral support.

"I'm sorry. My family is big and overwhelming. We just came in here and took over," I offer my apology.

"No! I love this. This is wonderful and it fills my heart. I love having your family here. I love making use of this big old house. That's why I always cook for the hands and invite them to stay. I love having people around. This house was built for this. When Ronan and I married, we planned on filling this house with kids but that just didn't happen for us. God blessed me with Nick and I'm so grateful. That's all I need. He's the light of my life and I'm so glad he found you and because of that I now have my big family. Thank you," she whispers and I feel my nose tingle. When Ronan makes his way to us he leans in and gives me a kiss on the cheek.

I start to walk away and give them privacy but Ronan calls my name. I kind of know what's coming so I put on my false attitude and sigh dramatically before I turn to face him. "Yes, Papa Ronan?" I ask sweetly and watch his lips tip at the ends, but he tries to hide it.

"You eat?" he asks but it's more of an order than a question.

I turn fully to him with my hands on my hips. "In the last five minutes? No. I'm still digesting the food your son piled on my plate thirty minutes ago. Think I'm good for another ten minutes or so. Thanks for asking though." I join Nick with a smile playing on my lips.

"Well, lunch is in about three hours and China's making Frito pies so you best get your skinny tail up here or else," he warns.

Now, the problem here is I want to argue with Ronan but I love Frito pies. Like really love them. Some people love a good steak, some love Belgian chocolate and others love a fine wine. Me, my perfect meal consists of a Bud Light and a big red, Frito pie and the only thing that could make it better is a second helping of Frito pie. I can eat Frito pies all day, every day just like my dad. It hits me, my dad. My dad and I had a tradition of eating Frito pies at my brothers' sporting events. When I was younger, if I were home from school sick, my dad would swing by the house at lunch and bring me a pie and a big red because oddly, those always made me better. Sometimes I'd hang out with my dad while he was working and go to job sites with him. Depending on what area of town we were in, we'd stop at the Hot Dog House or Hot Joy and get us a pie. I search the room for him and see him sitting at the table watching me joke around with Ronan. There's an air of sadness to him and I frown. I wrap my arms around his neck from behind and kiss his bearded cheek, feeling his breath hitch. "Daddy, you giving away our secrets?" I ask softly.

"Just trying to make sure you'll be okay, baby girl," he answers. *Oh, my God, He's going to make me cry.* He kisses me on the cheek. "Love you. Just want you happy. Leaving soon and I just want you taken care of," he says but his voice trails off, full of emotion. He better not cry, because I will absolutely lose it. Ronan's eyes have gone soft as well.

"I'll bring my skinny tail up for lunch," I tell him in all sincerity. He smiles and nods as I give my dad another hug. He pats my arms and then stands and leaves the room. My mom gives me a sad smile but nods and mouths, *he'll be okay,* before following him into the other room. A stranger who looks at my dad will see a man over six feet tall, huge like a grizzly bear. His beard and hair passed his collar, throw in his loud foul mouth and they'd never know the heart of gold that lies beneath all that. Jaycee loops her arms through mine as we watch their exit.

Right as I'm about break down in emotional sobs, Red calls out to Nick. "It's time. Shelly's ready."

"Let's go, then," Nick says to Huck and Levi as he heads for the door. He looks back at me. "Want to come?" he asks.

"Absolutely," I say and go for my coat.

"Hey, what's going on?" Star asks.

"Shelly's about to deliver." Huck replies.

"I want to go," Darcy says her and Levi join us.

"Me too," Star says.

"Max?" Jaycee asks and Blue walks over and grabs both their coats.

Before I know it, everyone in the room has walked over and is grabbing their coats. My uncle Brock is squatting down in front of Callie and zipping up her puffy pink snow coat. Today our little fashion diva has her hair in a ponytail and is wearing little brown and pink timberland hiking boots over her faded blue jeans and a brown fuzzy sweater. When I think my uncle is about to pull her coats hood over her head, instead he pulls a small pink camo John Deere cap from his back pocket and tucks it on her head and then pulls her pony tail through the closure on the back. When she bends her head way back at look at him over the brim of her cap, he starts laughing. She walks to Linc keeping her head way back so she can see where she's going and a round of chuckles can be heard when she struggles to see. The cap is blocking her view like blinders on a horse. I'm thinkin' my uncle did that on purpose. She reaches Linc and lifts her arms up to be picked up. Yes, our little princess shall not be walking today. Linc picks her up and pushes her hat back a little and she giggles.

"Better?" he asks. When she nods, she bops him in the face and he starts cracking up. My aunt hands him some mittens for her, but Delta takes them and puts them on while my aunt pulls on her coat. All the while Callie's silver starry eyes are watching her.

"You're pretty," Callie tells Delta.

"Thank you." Delta says.

"Are you my aunt too?" she asks excitedly. Linc cuts in before Delta can reply.

"No, honey. You know I'm your brother, right?" Linc asks her and she nods. He dodges the brim of her cap, laughing. "Well, after Delta and I get married, she's going to be your sister-in-law," he says grinning, knowing she won't really understand but Callie eyes draw together while she's thinking and whether or not she really understands, I don't know. But it's enough to cause her to jump in his arms. "Sister?" Delta's face lights up in smile when she nods. "Yippee," Callie squeals making everyone happy for them.

"Where do they find these outfits?" I ask no one but look over at Nick. "I want a baby. A girl. Like, now," I say in total seriousness.

"Alright then, let's get hitched as soon as possible but in the meantime, since you placed your order, we'll start on that too," he winks.

"Um, did you say get hitched, Nick?" I ask and he freezes.

"Oh, I'm sorry darlin'. I mean married. Betrothed to one another or something romantic like that," he says and pulls me to him.

"No, Nick. I'm fine with hitched. Call me your ball and chain, I don't care. But you want to marry me?" I ask feeling a bit emotional.

"Well, damn, Abigail. What do you think? I mean, what do you think we're doing here?" He grins while taking in my shock. "Darlin', of course I want to marry you. Tomorrow, today even. I just didn't want to rush you while you were finishing up school. I planned on popping the question right after you graduated," he explains as he leans down and kisses me. We kiss for a few moments before I hear throats being cleared. A blush spreads across my cheeks when I realize everyone saw us but that fades when I look back up at Nick.

"Baby, I love you," I tell him and bury my face in Nick's neck.

"Love you too."

"Anyone else want to announce they're getting married before we head down to barn?" Ronan asks in fake annoyance.

"Ronan!" China scolds.

"Well, I'm just saying, Blue and Jaycee, Levi and Darcy, Linc and Delta and now Nick and Abigail. I'm just putting it out there," he says and raises his hands in defeat.

"Star?" Huck asks carefully. "Don't you think we should—"

"Yes!" Star blurts out causing the room to laugh and Huck's eyes to widen in fear and shock. Star takes his look in and then panics. "Oh, my God, that's not what you were going to ask me is it? Oh, I need to go. I'm sorry. It's okay. Forget I said that," she mumbles her face red in embarrassment and eyes full of tears as she looks around the room. She rushes over to the table where her car keys and purse are and grabs them and starts for the door. I start to cry for her but when Nick walks over to Huck and pops him in the back of the head. I gasp in shock.

"She finally says yes and you fucking forget how to talk and move," Nicks teases.

"Language, Nick!" China scolds.

"Sorry, Mom," Nicks says and laughs when Huck finally blinks.

"She said yes?" he asks Nick and then looks around the room and sees everyone nodding. "Star?" Huck yells out right as she reaches the door. She turns around slowly but keeps her head down and I can hear her sniffling. "Come here, please."

"It's okay. I'm sorry, Huck. I just thought—" She doesn't move from her spot.

"Honey, please, come here," Huck repeats and they move towards each other. "Star," Huck says breathlessly. "I'm sorry." Star's breath hitches and more tears falls. "I don't have your ring with me. It's at the cabin," he reaches out and grabs her hands. "I've been planning this day for thirteen years and thought it would go different," he confesses.

"What?" Star asks, shocked. "You've been planning this?" she asks in disbelief.

"Since the day I kissed you behind the scoreboard. You've been mine ever since," he tells her.

"You want to marry me?" she asks softly.

"Let's go to the cabin so I can give you your ring."

"You got me a ring?" she asks as she closes the distance between them and wraps him in her arms.

"Ten years ago," he replies.

"What?"

"I bought you a ring ten years ago. Been waiting all this time to have it on your finger," he answers as he wraps her into his arms too.

"It's about time I should be wearing it, don't you think?" she asks and gives him a small smile.

"Past time," he replies as he breaks their embrace and pulls her out the door behind him.

Everyone is quiet as we listen to the truck doors slam and then the engine roar to life. As I hear the gravel crunching beneath the truck tires, I smile and take Nick's hand. It's quiet until I hear my dad speak to Ronan and everyone starts laughing.

"You did ask," my dad says.

"I did. Yes. I guess I did," Ronan says, defeated.

CHAPTER FORTY-THREE

We arrive at the barn and head for the stall where Dr. Tobin is standing with Dawson. His eyes go wide at seeing us all walking towards him. He chuckles to himself before giving a chin jerk.

"How she's doing?" Nick asks.

"Any minute. She's doing just fine. Handling it like a pro," he replies while introductions are made and handshakes are going on. "I'll stand by but doubt she'll need any of us. She's settling and nature is doing its thing. We just all need to be very quiet. Don't want to make her agitated," he tells us and we all nod in understanding.

"Callie? Want to see?" Nick asks and she nods but he doesn't take her from Linc. He moves so they can step forward and peek in the stall. When she sees Shelly laying there she lets out a little gasp and Linc put his finger to his mouth. "Shhh." She leans in close to his ear and whispers so loudly we all hear her.

"Linc that's a horsey. A pwetty horsey. Is she sweeping?"

"No honey, she's going to have a baby," Linc tells her.

"A baby?" she whispers excitedly but then she frowns. "A baby like me? Was I born in a horsey? How was I born in a horsey?" she asks in total seriousness looking back and forth between the horse and Linc. That does it. China, Violet, Lina, my grandma and Aunt Paige all walk quickly out of the barn trying to hold in their laughter.

Linc looks over at Delta. "I did that wrong, didn't I?" he asks, confused and Delta nods and laughs softly. "Um, here. You explain." He hands Callie to her daddy.

"Oh yeah, thanks a lot, Linc," my uncle says irritated and then looks at Callie in fear. "No, honey. See there's this big bird called the stork…" he begins and his voice trails off as he walks out of the barn most likely to give her to her mom.

Jaycee and I are trying to keep our laughs quiet but that was pretty funny. All the men and Kore and Allison are standing around the stall watching Shelly. There's a gushing sound and all the men gag and run out of the barn. Allison and Kore follow them while trying to hold in their laughs at their reaction. Nick's laughing silently but so hard he can't breathe.

"Her water broke," he tells me. The girls and I step forward; in time to we see a tiny horse leg coming out of Shelly. Someone has wrapped up her tail and she's bucking and grunting while laying down and stretching her legs out. I stare in awe as the front legs and then a head and then body makes its way out. Shelly lays back down and rests before giving a final grunt and then all of her foal is out. *Oh, my God.* Right after that, Shelly stands and goes to her baby and begins cleaning it. Aunt Paige comes back with Callie walking beside her, holding her hand.

"Come here, honey," Red says, and of course no problem, tattoos and all she goes right to him. He picks her up and lets her peek in the stall. Her eyes bug out and she points.

"Mommy. Baby," she whispers.

My aunt smiles. "Yes, that's her baby, Callie," she says.

With humor in her eyes Darcy chimes in. "You'll be doing that soon, Delta."

Delta's eyes fly to Darcy and she looks terrified. "The hell I will." She glares at Linc. "No!" she says and walks off with Linc following her, laughing.

For the next few minutes, we watch as the foal attempts to stand. It makes Callie giggle as she cheers the foal on. "Come on, baby horsey. You can do it," she encourages.

"What are you going to name her?" I ask Nick.

"Don't know yet," he replies. "What do you think, Callie?" he asks her.

She looks down as the foal tried to stand again and finally takes its feet only to fall again.

"Wobbles. Cause she wobbles," she laughs.

Nick looks at his Dad and who shrugs. "Wobbles it is then." Nick announces.

We all hang out for a little bit watching Shelly and Wobbles but all too soon it's time for everyone to hit the road and head back to San Antonio.

CHAPTER FORTY-FOUR

We all say our goodbyes and I can't lie, as I stand watching my family get in their vehicles and mount their bikes, my heart breaks a little. I know my mom and dad can sense it and are trying to make it easier on me so they leave first, but only after making plans with Nick's parents to come down to San Antonio for Christmas. Dawson offers to watch the ranch for a few days so everyone can go down. Having that planned makes me feel a little better but not enough to change my mood as I watch my brothers get in their cars. Jesse and Allison are quietly arguing before he reaches out, surprising her and tickling her until she drops the keys. Something is cooking fast there, I think and smile as they get in her car and start down the road. Jake climbs in his truck and Korea her rental. They're making a quick stop in town to turn in her car at the airport before hitting the road together. Nash and Chase are almost ready to go and are loading up their saddlebags. I try to smile as best I can when Chase looks over at me, but it's more wobbly than Wobbles. He comes over to me for one last hug.

"Abigail, it's only going to be seven days until you see us all again. Okay?" he tells me and I'll I can do is nod. He gives me a quick kiss on the forehead and without looking back straddles his bike and follows Nash down the road. Maybe he's emotional too. It's the first time the two of us have really been separate.

Uncle Brock and Aunt Paige are next, and after Callie says goodbye to Linc, Lina, Delta and Red she comes and gives me a big hug. She proceeds to give everybody else a hug before going back to my uncle Brock. Uncle Brock tugs me into a one arm hug.

"I'm proud of you. You're a strong girl. See you soon. Love you," he says. Again, I watch as they load up and with a final wave, drive off. Acer, Ana, Johnny and Blue are standing together chatting so I make my way to them and we all exchange hugs. Ana tells us she'll make a big batch of lumpia and bring it for Christmas dinner.

Jaycee embraces me in a hard, tight hug and my emotions finally break and I start to cry. "Going to miss you," she says in my ear.

"Me too," I whisper back.

Nick clears his throat, and I'm shocked to see he's holding one of my suitcases. "Darlin', you're breaking my heart. Listen, I think you should go home with your family for a few days. I don't like seeing you this sad and upset. I won't keep you here if you're not happy. I'll come down in a few days," he tells me and hands Blue the bag.

I stare at him and a new round of tears fall at the thought of leaving him behind. I'm not going anywhere.

"I'm not leaving you, Nick." I take my bag from Blue and set it down. "I love you. I'm going to be your ball and chain. We just kind of got somewhat engaged earlier, didn't we?" I ask and he nods. "Honeysuckle, I'm sad but I'm also happy. This is my life now. You're my life now. I'm never leaving you again." I slam my body into his. We hold each other tight as Darcy, Levi, Delta and Linc say their goodbyes and Nick's parents head back in the house. Finally, it's down to Jaycee, Blue, Nick and I and we're all waiting for someone to make the move.

"We're going. See you in seven days. Seven, Abigail," Blue says and I nod. "We're not a world apart. Five hours at the most. It takes that long to get to the damn mall from our home going down the highway," he says and he's right.

That puts it in total perspective for me and I give him and Jaycee one last hug before they head out. I watch them go and right before they get out of view something catches my eyes as it makes its way through the tall grass. It's the damn armadillo. It glances over at me and then wiggles across the road to the other side.

"Of course. There's no cars so it travels in warp speed across the road," I complain to Nick and shake my head. I go back to the cabin where Buford and Elvis have been sitting and I crouch down and give them some hugs and love before heading inside.

"After being in the barn all morning, I need a shower darlin'," Nick says. "Want to join me?" he asks as he carries my bag back in the house.

"I can't believe you packed my bag and wanted me to go," I tell him, a little hurt and disappointed. He turns my face to his and kisses me.

"First, I wasn't letting you go and never will. Second, if you would have left, I would have hopped in my truck and followed you down there. Third, that bag has nothing in it. It's completely empty. You're not getting away again, Abigail."

Thank God is my only thought as we close the door to our bedroom.

CHAPTER FORTY-FIVE

Standing in the shower washing Nick under the warm water, our need for one another grows. Stepping out, we only half dry off before walking to the bed. I sit on the side and wait but when Nick's phone rings, I nod and tell him to take it. While he's gone, I return to the bathroom and sit down at the vanity and begin to towel dry my hair. The door opens, and Nick joins me wearing nothing but his towel. Our eyes follow each other in the mirror until he's standing in front of me.

"Everything okay?" I ask as I lick my lips, my eyes taking in his body.

"Yes, all is good with Shelly and Wobbles so the vet is heading out." He steps closer to me. I realize I haven't heard half of what he said as I'm staring at his chest. Reaching up, I run my hands up his chest and back down his ribs until I reach his towel at his waist and I pull it open and let it fall to the ground. I lean in and kiss his abs, slowly making my way down. After exploring him with my hands, I take him in my mouth.

He jolts, cusses and gathers my hair into a ponytail with his hand, using it to control my movements. I moan every time his grip tightens. Feeling his dominance and control is turning me on and making me squirm. Nick lets me be me but then there's these moments, when he takes total control and I concede and give my surrender. He swells in my mouth and his grip on my hair tightens so I place my hands on his abs, they're like stone. I know he's close as I get a small taste of him. He tries to pull away but I grab his hips and pull him forward again.

"Darlin' if you're going to do this, take all of me, Abigail, you understand?" he demands and I look up. I nod as he grips my hair, pulling him from me before coming forward again. "Open," he demands. *Shit, that's hot.* He's watching me intently and I whimper. I take him as deep as I can but it's not enough. He assumes complete control and holds my head still as he moves in out of my mouth. He lets out a deep growl and then his taste fills my mouth and I take him all just as he demanded.

His breathing calms and his grip on my hair finally loosens. He surprises me when all of a sudden I'm up and out of the chair. He sits me on the vanity and then his mouth is on me, returning the gesture. Now, I hold his head where I want it as he takes me where I need to go. Using his mouth and fingers he sends me into a powerful orgasm that leaves me seeing stars. He holds me until my shudders stop and then helps me off the vanity and walks us over to the dresser. I grab one of his shirts when his demanding voice reaches me.

"No. Not done." He bends me forward to lay my upper body across the top. The stone is cold against my naked body but the only chills are from him standing close behind me. 'Darlin', do you remember taunting me with Blue?" he asks, while rubbing his hands along my back and hips.

"Honeysuckle, I wasn't taunting you. He's like my—" before I can say brother there's a smack and I feel a slight sting. Okay, so this is *not* going to get me to stop talking to other men. As a matter of fact, Nick's encouraging it without even realizing it.

"He's not your brother, darlin'."

"What about Red?" He growls and I earn another smack, and then another. I lower my head and moan but also to try and hide my smile. Now for the grand finale

"And Levi, Huck?" I ask softly, squirming in anticipation.

Nick leans down across my naked body, his hands gripping my hips, "Abigail, imagine this." he spanks me a few more times on each side before coming back over my squirming body. "Only being tied down," he whispers against my back as he starts trailing kisses down my spine while his fingers find me and begin spreading my wetness around, preparing me.

As he kisses and bites his way back up, between my moans I tell him, "Nick, your threats? You're doing it wrong," I whisper breathlessly.

He taps my legs apart with his knee and then slowly enters me only a little at a time. His thrusts are slow and shallow, slowly building. "Am I, fire?" he asks against my shoulder before nipping it.

"Are you what, baby?" I ask, not understanding anything anymore.

He chuckles. "Am I doing it wrong, Abigail?"

Oh. I kind of remember saying that. "Nick, honeysuckle, you're doing it right. So perfectly right." I turn my head and kiss him. When I feel I'm close, I close my eyes and lower my head, but Nick pulls it back by my hair. He holds my head up by my ponytail so he can see me.

"Want to see. Keep your eyes open, Abigail," he demands and that's it. I let out a scream and tighten around him. I watch in the reflection of the mirror as he struggles to keep going deep around my muscles convulsing. When I finally relax, he begins powering into me like never before. I'm on the edge again and right before we both come, I meet his eyes in the mirror. "I love you."

CHAPTER FORTY-SIX

After dinner, Nick tells me he has to run down and get some more firewood just down the hill. I tell him I'll stay behind and unpack but when I run across my baby blue bikini I decide I'm going to try out the heated pool. I change, grab a towel and slip on my boots for the short walk across the deck. I smile when I see the clear water illuminated by the underwater lights and reflecting against the moon in the sky.

I drop my towel on the chair and spot a stereo sitting within the wall of the deck along with built-in speakers. How cool is that? I turn it on and Fuel's *Hemorrhage* fills the air around me. I pull off my boots and walk into the water and when I feel its warmth, I sink in. Moving my arms in long relaxed stokes, I swim towards the deep end and stop when I get to edge. Resting my elbows on the edge, I can just make out small flickering lights off in the distance. I know some of those are the cabins and some the barns and shelters. Everyone and everything must be asleep because the night is quiet and peaceful. This is Heaven.

I slip underneath the water, wet my hair, pushing it from my face as I break through the surface. The stars are shining brighter than I've ever seen there's so many and some are twinkling brighter than others. The clouds have cleared and the temperature is rising back into the high 60's. It's the most beautiful night. I float on my back while looking at the stars, lounging peacefully, the music muffled by the water covering everything but my face. It vaguely registers that the song has stopped but then I hear Life House, *You and Me* start playing and I smile but don't move. I feel the slight waves of the water and then arms go around me and pull me up. I open my eyes when my body becomes flush with Nick's and no words are shared as I wrap my arms around his neck and my legs around his waist. We float in silence with only the slight touch of his hands rubbing my back and mine play with his hair at his neck, our movements not even causing a ripple in the water.

Out of nowhere, I think about what Nick said about his mom. "She gave me the words I needed to turn back and run to you." I lay my head against his shoulder. "Baby, what did your mom say to you the night you almost walked away that had you turning back?" I ask quietly.

"I was in bad shape. She said she'd never heard me like this. Torn. Hurting," he answers, drawing me closer and deeper into the warm water. "I told her I wasn't sure what I was doing and she asked me what would make me sure. I told her we needed time. When she asked me what we needed time for, I told her we needed time to fall in love." he tells me, pausing to take a breath. "How long does it take someone to fall in love? When she asked me that, I took some time and thought about her question. I started back to the hospital entrance after telling her what I already knew, and I suspect she knew as well. I was already in love with you. That's when I ran back to you. Abigail, I will always run back to you. I love you." His lips touch mine in a tender kiss.

"I love you too, Nick."

PLAYLIST

Boogie Shoes - KC and the Sunshine Band

George Strait- The Chair

I Will Survive - Gloria Gaynor

She's Country - Jason Aldean

Let It Go - James Bay

Take My Drunk Ass Home - Luke Bryan

How Country Feels - Randy Houser

Hemorrhage - Fuel

You And Me - Lifehouse

ACKNOWLEDGEMENTS

To my readers,

I can't tell you how much you mean to me. To be able to share something so dear to me and have it become dear to you too is something I can't explain. You crying when I cry, laughing when I laugh, loving and hating just like me, it's goes to a level so high it's unreachable.

Without you, Jaycee and Max, Rocky and all the McGinty's, they wouldn't be. I can't imagine them not being so thank you from the bottom of my heart.

As always I want to thank my wonderful family.

Dennis, my kids, Patrick, Regan and Julia, Jenny, Marcus and Walter, my grandchildren, Jacob, Wesley and Marci Rae, my parents, Ben and Judy, the Schooleys-Uncle Chuck and Aunt Bev, Uncle Wayne and Aunt Linda, Aunt Donna, Uncle Buzz and Aunt Grace, my mom, Darla-RIP, Laura and Sam, Zara, my parents-in-law, Larry and Anatalia without you none of this would be possible. Thank you for loving and supporting me.

To all my amazing friends and family in San Antonio, thank you for believing in me and buying my books. It's good to be home!

GO BEARS GO!

Texas! I love you!

Fort Belvoir Exchange family—I miss you and can still feel your support 1,500 miles away. You're amazing.

Virginia friends—I miss you! Thank you for buying and reading my books.

Cassia—I laugh because you are the most amazing and patient person and still, I know I drive you crazy. Thank you for being so awesome and understanding.

Judi—You're amazing. Simply amazing.

Concierge Literary Promotions—Judi and Alissa, thank you for your beautiful work.

To all authors—thank you for always uplifting new authors and being encouraging.

Thank you for inspiring me.

I want to thank Lance Jones and Cassia Brightmore for being my Nick and Abigail. You two are perfect and I'm over the moon you were kind enough to grace my cover.